PLAIN OUTSIDER

ALISON STONE

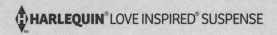

HARLEQUIN® LOVE INSPIRED® SUSPENSE

Recycling programs
for this product may
not exist in your area.

 LOVE INSPIRED BOOKS

ISBN-13: 978-1-335-49037-7

Plain Outsider

www.Harlequin.com

Printed in U.S.A.

A flush of dread she couldn't explain washed over her as she made her way through the parking garage.

She quickened her steps and glanced over her shoulder. The deck was empty, but her imagination was full of all sorts of crazy notions.

It's just the stress.

When she reached the truck, she clicked the unlock button this time and heard a *click-click*. She reached for the door handle when footsteps rushed toward her. Before she had a chance to react, a solid body slammed her into the side of the truck. Pain ripped through her hip and ribs.

She opened her mouth to scream when a hand clamped over her mouth, making it impossible.

"You're dead," a deep voice growled.

As terror shot through her veins, the words of the bishop came slamming back into her brain, a cautionary warning she had refused to heed.

There is evil in the outside world. We must remain separate.

Becky should have listened. It was time for her to pay for her sins.

Alison Stone lives with her husband of more than twenty years and their four children in Western New York. Besides writing, Alison keeps busy volunteering at her children's schools, driving her girls to dance and watching her boys race motocross. Alison loves to hear from her readers at Alison@AlisonStone.com. For more information, please visit her website, alisonstone.com. She's also chatty on Twitter, @alison_stone. Find her on Facebook at Facebook.com/alisonstoneauthor.

The Lord is my strength and my shield;
my heart trusted in him, and I am helped:
therefore my heart greatly rejoiceth;
and with my song will I praise him.
–Psalms 28:7

To Mom, with love

ONE

The headlights on Deputy Becky Spoth's patrol car illuminated the lines on the deserted country road. Some of her fellow deputies complained about the overnight shift, but Becky had grown to like it. There was something calming about patrolling the quiet roads devoid of cars or horses, or more important, people. It gave her a lot of time for quiet reflection while still providing a means to pay the mortgage. She appreciated her job now more than ever when just a few days ago she wondered if she'd ever be out on patrol again.

That was the thing about this job. Things could change on a dime. The radio that had been silent most of her shift suddenly crackled to life as if to prove her point. "Report of a break-in on Robin Nest Road. How far away are you, Deputy Spoth?"

She didn't have to give the location a moment's thought. She had grown up in Quail Hollow and knew all the windy roads and farms, even the ones the town didn't see fit to mark. That was the thing about a small town. Everyone knew everything about everything and everyone.

"I'm a mile out." Despite a year as a deputy, her

stomach bottomed out and her mouth grew dry. Would she ever get used to answering calls, especially alone at night? All the officers in the sheriff's department traveled solo, but backup was usually only a moment away.

Backup. More than once over the past couple weeks, she wished she hadn't been the first to arrive to help Deputy Ned Reich subdue a young Amish man, an incident that had turned the sheriff's department upside down.

Had turned the small town of Quail Hollow, New York, upside down.

Forcing the distracting thoughts out of her mind, Becky weighed the pros and cons of turning on the patrol car's lights and siren. She didn't want to give the possible intruder a heads-up that a sheriff's deputy was on the way, a chance to get away. But she didn't want to surprise some unsuspecting driver. She stretched across to the control panel. *Flick.* Lights. No siren.

The engine revved under the weight of her foot on the accelerator. The power of the patrol car never failed to impress her, especially for a woman who didn't get her driver's license until she was twenty-five.

The first hints of pink and purple pushed into the black night sky as she drove toward Robin Nest. The only homes out this way belonged to the Amish. Perhaps a young Amish boy had been sneaking home after a night of shenanigans. A lot of the Amish youth went to Sunday singings and for some, the fun stretched into the early morning with unsuspecting parents who might glance outside at the most inopportune time and mistake their son for an intruder.

But that raised the question: Who called the sheriff? The Amish preferred not to deal with law enforcement. And there was the issue of a phone, but even Becky realized that some Amish were adapting to the modern world by allowing phones and cell phones in a limited capacity. Like a landline in a barn or a cell phone strictly for work purposes. She doubted she'd be seeing an Amish family sitting around the table at the diner in town all staring at their cell phones anytime soon. A bit of a slippery slope, all the same.

As Becky's patrol car crested the hill, the headlights from an oncoming car blinded her. Instinctively, she jammed on the brakes as the approaching car veered into her lane. She gripped the wheel tightly and braced for impact, a prayer crossing her lips.

The tires skidded on the pavement. She swerved. The patrol car careened off the road and plowed into the nearby field, stalks of corn slapping at her windshield, her entire body jostling. The vehicle finally came to a hard stop and her seat belt dug into her chest. She let out a breath on a whoosh and slumped into the leather seat. She pried her fingers from the steering wheel and thanked God she was in one piece.

She contacted dispatch with her current predicament, then released the seat belt. She pushed open the door against the corn stalks. With heightened awareness, she stepped out into the field, her boots sinking into the soft soil. Her first concern was the other driver. Had he had a medical issue? Was he drunk?

The night air smelled thick, the combination of rich soil and burned rubber. She squinted against the glare of the red and blue patrol lights.

Plodding through the soil, she pushed the cornstalks out of the way. The other vehicle had stopped, positioned across the road, its extinguished headlights pointed toward her. A shadow of a figure sat motion-less in the driver's seat.

Is he watching me?

"Hello, are you okay?" she called, nerve endings prickling to life. Where was her backup?

The headlights flipped on and her hand instinctively came up to block the bright beams trained on her.

"Turn your headlights off, sir." She cocked her head, straining to see past the blinding lights.

The high beams flashed on and she jerked her head back. *What in the world?*

Her other hand hovered over her gun. *You've got this. You're trained for this.* She took a step back. Crops didn't exactly provide protection, but they could provide a hiding place if necessary.

"Step out of your car," she ordered, keeping her tone authoritative and even, like she had practiced. Becky was jacked up on adrenaline from nearly getting hit head-on, but the mood had shifted from apprehension to determination. She had a job to do.

The man was watching her. Toying with her. She planted her feet in the soil, ready to draw her gun. Her legs felt like jelly, but she ignored the sensation. Nerves came with the job. She had been trained to fire a gun and hit a target. She had never shot another human being and prayed tonight wouldn't change that.

"Out of your car now!" she ordered, feeling her entire body tense.

The engine of the car fired to life, the sound rumbling through her chest. The tires spun, spewing the acrid smell of burned rubber. She fought back a cough, keeping her sharpened attention on the vehicle. The tires gained purchase and the car backed up, stopped abruptly, then raced down the road, back in the direction it had come.

Becky's shoulders sagged and she drew in a few deep breaths. Staring toward the vehicle, she waited a moment, anticipating another drive-by. The early-morning chirping of birds seeped into her consciousness before she allowed herself to let down her guard. *He's gone.* She strode back to the patrol car and flipped off the flashing lights. She pressed her shoulder radio and said, "ETA on the tow truck?"

"Five minutes," the dispatcher asked. "Everything okay?"

"Yeah," she said, a not-exactly truthful reply, but a necessary one. A person couldn't show weakness on this job. Not if they wanted to be seen as competent.

Becky gave the dispatcher what limited information she had on the car that ran her off the road. Maybe they'd pull him over, figure out what his problem was.

Becky leaned against the trunk of her patrol car and ran a hand across her clenched jaw. She didn't know who ran her off the road, but she suspected he had known exactly who his target was.

Her.

This wasn't exactly how Becky had envisioned her first shift back at work. The tow truck driver insisted he could drop her off in front of the sheriff's station before taking the vehicle to the repair shop to make sure mud from her off-roading adventure wasn't clogging anything up. She was pretty sure he had been more specific with some technical terms, but she had tuned him out after the second time he appeared to be hitting on her. Like that never happened before: a guy hitting on a female sheriff's deputy.

Sorry, not interested.

"Stop. I'm going to get out here," Becky said, growing impatient as he debated with himself whether he'd be able to weave the tow truck through the narrow parking lot adjacent to the employee entrance.

"No problem." The young man stopped and gave her a silent stare while she scooted out of the cab. Her foot didn't reach the ground and she almost missed the running board, which would have added insult to injury. It wasn't exactly a good shift when a deputy returned with her patrol car trailing behind her.

She didn't bother giving the tow truck driver instructions because she suspected her boss already had. After determining that his deputy was okay and that the call on Robin Nest was a false alarm, the sheriff had instructed her to report to his office the minute she returned.

On solid ground, Becky smoothed out her uniform shirt. She watched as the tow truck lumbered away, its engine chugging as the sun poked over the horizon. The day shift deputies had started to arrive.

Just great.

Becky might have been imagining it, but several seemed to give her the side eye as they strolled toward the employee entrance, and she suspected it had nothing to do with her going four-wheeling in the cornfields with a patrol car.

She sighed heavily. She had hoped her first day back on patrol was going to be a smooth transition after a rough week. Apparently not.

Fighting the urge to fidget with the cuffs of her

sleeves, she approached the entrance. She had wanted to go straight home, take a hot bath and get some solid sleep. But she had strict instructions to report to the sheriff.

Becky walked at a steady pace. She squared her shoulders, determined to prove to anyone who might be judging her that she was confident and self-assured, despite the mud caked up in the wheel wells of her vehicle. She frowned, realizing her driving abilities weren't the only thing her fellow officers would be questioning. Several had voiced their displeasure when she filed her official report last week against a fellow officer who had been placed on a long-term suspension while the department continued their investigation.

The memory of the sudden brightness of the headlights blinding her earlier this morning while she stood in the cornfields knotted her stomach. Could the anger of one of her fellow officers have turned to retribution? To show Becky just how wrong she had been to point a finger at another officer? To make sure she knew her place not only as one of the newer deputies, but also as a woman?

Support fellow deputies. Don't testify against them.

Someone had left that note for her last week on her windshield, but she didn't think it applied in this case. She couldn't ignore when a fellow deputy crossed a line.

She brushed at her white uniform sleeves, convincing herself that yes, she had done the right thing. A law-enforcement officer didn't have the right to beat up a young man, even if he had led him on a high-speed chase, barely missing a child crossing the street after getting the mail.

Becky slowed, allowing the first rays of morning sun to warm her face and the buzz of her nerves to settle a bit. An arm reached around her and grabbed the handle of the station door, surprising her.

"Oh, sorry," Becky muttered, not realizing she had been blocking the entrance. She glanced up into the serious face of Deputy Harrison James, the only deputy with less time at the Quail Hollow Sheriff's Department than she had. But she wasn't naive to assume his lack of time in this department meant he had less experience. Everything about him screamed skill, confidence and an "I don't care what anyone thinks of me" vibe. Three qualities Becky admired.

Three qualities she would like to purchase in bushels right now. If only that was a one-click option online.

Harrison nodded in a silent greeting and pulled open the door for her. He was standing so close she could see the flecks of yellow in his brown eyes.

"Thank you." Becky averted her gaze and stepped through the door and he followed behind her. The brief exchange had probably been the longest one she'd had with Deputy James. He wasn't exactly the chatty type. More like tall, dark and brooding. Considering the mood she was in of late, she could relate.

"No problem," he said, his voice low and gruff. They walked slowly across the small lobby, waiting to be admitted into the secure office area. Deputy James frowned as he pressed the buzzer. He looked like a man who hadn't had his morning coffee. But at least he hadn't had the kind of morning she'd had.

The interior door buzzed, and Harrison once again opened the door for her. "Tough shift?" His comment startled her.

"Um, yeah." Heat fired in her cheeks as she smiled meekly and jabbed her thumb in the general direction of where she'd climbed out of the tow truck. "Someone ran me off the road."

His brow furrowed. "Did he stop?"

"At first, but he took off once I got out of the vehicle."

Harrison looked like he was going to say more when Becky heard a stern voice calling her name.

"Looks like the sheriff's looking for me."

The corners of her fellow deputy's lips turned down. "Don't let me hold you up."

Reflexively, Becky checked her collar, making sure her uniform was in place. Sheriff Thomas Landry tapped the door frame before disappearing back inside his office. No deputy made the sheriff call them twice.

Becky forced a cheery demeanor for Anne Wagner, the sheriff's administrative assistant, as she passed. They had been peers before Becky had finished her training and become a deputy. Anne raised her eyebrows and returned a smile, a cross between friendship and *I hope everything's okay*. No one liked to be on the new sheriff's bad side. He had only been elected six months ago, and by all accounts, he was tough. All his officers toed the line or paid the price.

Exhibit one: Deputy Ned Reich, the deputy Becky had testified against.

"Good morning, Sheriff." Becky lingered in the doorway, hoping this would be a quick chat along the lines of "How was your first day back?"

"You've had better mornings, I'm sure," the sheriff responded, his tone calm and even. In the short time she had worked with him, he seemed unflappable.

As cool as his demeanor in the ubiquitous political commercials that littered the airways: "Vote for me, Thomas Landry, for sheriff. The kind of transparent leader Quail Hollow needs." The department was still trying to reshape its image after one of their own had been convicted in a twenty-year-old murder of a young Amish mother.

"Yes, but it's all part of the job," she said. "Anyone find the car?"

"We haven't located the vehicle that ran you off the road yet, but everyone has the description."

"It was hard to see. Sedan. Early model. Maybe a B in the license plate. Isn't very descriptive, I know, but it was dark."

He waved his hand. "Glad you're okay. Probably some punk on a dare. Turns out the call to Robin Nest was a dead end, too." He shook his head. "Like we have nothing better to do than respond to crank calls."

"You think someone was dared to play chicken with a patrol car?" Becky asked in disbelief.

The sheriff leaned back and crossed his arms. "Or someone had too much to drink. Or maybe someone thought our country roads would make a great speedway. Easy to lose control." He shrugged. "We'll get to the bottom of it."

Still standing in the doorway, she glanced over her shoulder. The deputies were still wandering in for the start of the day shift. "I'm not exactly the most popular person around here." But how could she suggest that one of her fellow deputies might be out to get her without sounding paranoid, or at the very least, like someone who wasn't a team player?

The moment to offer a possible culprit passed and

the sheriff gestured at her to come farther into his office. "Close the door."

Becky's heart sank. *Close the door.* Nothing good was ever said behind closed doors, unless it involved a raise or a promotion, neither of which she was in line for.

"I'm afraid I have bad news," the sheriff said.

TWO

"Bad news?" What more could possibly go wrong?

Sitting behind his mahogany desk, the sheriff forced a tight smile and held his hand out to Becky. "Have a seat."

Becky wanted to refuse the seat, hoping that whatever he had to tell her could be said while she was standing, but her knees felt warm and wobbly. Swallowing hard, she moved around to the front of the chair and lowered herself into the seat as he requested. "What's going on?" She hoped her crossed ankles, hands politely folded on her lap and her square shoulders exuded outward confidence. Inside she felt like puking.

The sheriff tapped the pads of his fingers together and seemed to be looking right through her, as if collecting his thoughts. "I know you've been having a hard time since the Elijah Lapp incident."

"Yes." Short of leaving her Amish family, the past week had been the hardest of her life. When she took the oath to uphold the law, she never thought it would include speaking out against one of her fellow deputies.

"You've been under tremendous pressure," the sheriff said with a reassuring tilt to his mouth.

"Yes." Becky swallowed hard, feeling a bit like she was being interrogated again. Like she had when she answered questions about The Incident. That was how she had begun to think of it. A young Amish man had led Deputy Ned Reich on a high-speed chase and only stopped when he bailed out of his car in the hopes of making a getaway on foot. Fueled by adrenaline and a well-known bad attitude, Deputy Reich had quickly caught up with the man and beaten him to within an inch of his life. By the time Becky—Reich's backup—arrived on the scene, the young Amish man was on the ground and Ned was driving his fist into his face. Becky had stared at the ceiling each night wondering what would have happened if she hadn't come by to put an end to the beating.

Even now she wondered how she had been able to stop the fight. The events of that afternoon blurred into an adrenaline-fueled haze. She thanked God she had the strength and inclination to do something.

Becky bent back her fingers on one hand in a nervous gesture. Once she became aware of it, she dropped her hand, only to absentmindedly pick it up and start again.

She had left the Amish because she felt like she had a bigger calling—to help people outside the small Amish community. But she was beginning to think this job was going to be the death of her. She never imagined small-town policing could be such stressful work.

The sheriff picked up a cell phone that had been face down on his desk, then put it back down again. "New evidence has come to light."

"New evidence against Deputy Reich?" A part of her was relieved. The more independent evidence against Ned, perhaps the less they'd have to rely on her testimony when it came to his trial. For now she had only testified in the confines of the department, providing enough information to keep Reich out of uniform for the foreseeable future. Maybe forever, depending on what additional evidence the sheriff had found. She hated this situation, but if she could find a spark of hope, this was it. Maybe her life would get back to normal and her fellow officers wouldn't treat her like a traitor.

The sheriff shot her a subtle gaze that chilled her to the core. She had misread this entire situation. "What is it?" Her body seemed to be hovering over her.

The sheriff touched the corner of his computer screen, adjusting its angle so she could see it. He clicked a few keys on his keyboard and a video frame popped up. The sheriff clicked the arrow button and an image of Ned pummeling the Amish kid while he was down on the pavement came into focus. The familiar uneasy feeling swept over her. The video had been taken from her dash cam on her patrol car. She wanted to look away, but didn't. *Couldn't.* There was a reason the sheriff was showing her this video, the same video she had seen play over and over again during her testimony against the man.

Her heart raced, just as it did the afternoon the events unfolded. Just as it did every time she had to relive the moment. She ran her hands up and down the arms of the chair. "I've seen this video more times than I can count, sir. Are we looking at something new?"

The sheriff cut her a quick gaze. "Hold on." He

moved the mouse and scanned over a few files. Perhaps he had shown her the wrong video. "Here it is."

This time when he clicked on the arrow, another video played. She slid to the edge of her seat as the familiar scene played out from a new angle. One she had never seen before. She shot a quick glance to her boss, then back to the video. This time she appeared on the screen. She had out her baton. Nausea swirled in her gut.

"Stop. Stop. Stop." Her terrified voice could be heard in the video. She had her baton raised, much like Ned had his fist raised moments ago in the other video.

"What is this?" Her voice cracked.

"Someone took a video with their cell phone."

She stared at the screen as if watching someone else. A million memories from that day assaulted her, but this particular one escaped her. As she approached, Ned dragged the man behind his patrol car. This was when her dash cam lost coverage. But this video caught more, like a second camera on a movie set. This time Becky could be seen marching toward where the two men had disappeared.

The sheriff stopped the video and pointed to a part with the tip of his pen. "What are you doing here?"

"Um—" she stared at the computer screen until it went blurry "—I'm raising my baton."

"What did you do with your baton?" The sheriff moved the pen away from the screen and covered the mouse with the palm of his hand. He clicked on Play. On the video, she was commanding that they stop.

Who? Her fellow officer? The man getting beat?

She blinked rapidly. "I needed to help…" The next word got caught in her throat. Did she need to help

Ned? Her fellow officer? Or had she been determined to save the young Amish man?

"Who were you going to help, Deputy Spoth?" He hit Pause again.

Becky sat ramrod straight on the edge of her seat and squared her shoulders. She had the answer. The question was easy, right? "I had to stop the fight. I had to get the driver safely into custody and away from Deputy Reich. The situation had turned out of control."

"Would you say you'd do whatever it took to stop the fight?"

"I'm not sure what you're asking." She flinched, then turned to stare at the screen, her digital form frozen with an anguished expression on her face. Becky may have been fairly naive because of her upbringing, but she studied people, knew how to respond. She was a quick learner and she wasn't going to allow the sheriff to get her to say something that could jeopardize her career.

The sheriff clicked Play. Video Becky walked authoritatively toward Reich's patrol car. She could be seen with her baton raised. To hit someone? Then she saw nothing.

On the video, someone muttered and then gravel came into view as the person took off running through what looked to be cornfields while still recording on their phone. Then the video came to a quick stop and the screen went black.

"I don't understand." A hot flush of dread blanketed her skin.

The sheriff sighed heavily and leaned back in his chair. It groaned under his weight. "This video was submitted to Deputy Reich's lawyer."

"Who?" The single word came out in a squeak. She cleared her throat. "Who turned it in? Why not turn it in to the department?"

"We're working on that. The lawyer said it was from an anonymous source. The witness claims you hit Elijah Lapp on the head with your baton, thus ending the fight and potentially leading to the young Amish man's cracked skull."

Cold dread washed over her and she thought she was going to be sick. "Wait…what? No. That's not…" The memories of that day were disjointed, but she didn't hit Elijah. No way.

"Deputy Spoth," the sheriff said in a soothing voice, but she was having none of it.

"This is all a misunderstanding. I didn't hit anyone with my baton. I used it to pry the men apart. That's why I had the baton out." It was all coming back to her now in a flood of formerly suppressed memories. Or was she grasping for the truth? Was she confused? Had she done something regrettable in the heat of the moment? She blinked slowly. The walls of the room closed in on her. She tugged on her collar. "You can ask Ned." As soon as the words spilled from her lips, she realized the futility of it. Why would Ned help her after she testified against him? Cost him his job? She looked up and met the sheriff's even gaze and knew she didn't stand a chance to talk her way out of this.

"Ned's lawyer insists that you landed the final blow that cracked Elijah Lapp's skull. Ned's lawyer provided the video."

"But…"

"Reich's been with the sheriff's department for twenty-five years." The sheriff glanced at the closed door behind her, as if to make sure he wouldn't be over-heard. "Between you and me, he's a hothead, but he's never gone this far."

"We can interview Elijah." Becky leaned forward on the edge of her chair, feeling like all the oxygen had been sucked from the room.

"Elijah has no memory of the incident." The sheriff's calm, cool demeanor only served to morph her initial fear to white-hot anger. "He's recovering at home and his family isn't allowing anyone from the sheriff's department to speak with him."

"I can't believe this."

The sheriff held up his hand. "I don't believe you hit the young man."

Hope straightened Becky's backbone, only for her to be immediately deflated with the sheriff's next words. "Despite what I think, I can't ignore this video. I ran for sheriff on the pledge that this office would be transparent and not allow any wrongdoing. This community has a reason to mistrust the sheriff's department after one of our own was arrested for murder."

Becky grew dizzy. "That was so long ago."

"But the perception that the sheriff's department protected him has hurt us." The sheriff shook his head. "We must regain the trust of the community."

"But—" Her world was sputtering out of control.

"Until we can clear you, you're suspended."

Becky stood to leave when the sheriff held out his hand.

"I'll need your gun and badge."

Deputy Harrison James climbed behind the wheel of his patrol car and turned the key in the ignition. He took a minute to adjust the AC vents, directing them toward his face. It was going to be a scorcher today. But hot in the country was never the same as hot in the city.

Fighting crime in the city was a whole new ball-game when the temperatures rose. Tempers spiked in direct proportion. And the concrete buildings held the heat. Here, the soft wind had a chance to reach a person across the large open spaces giving him time to think before he threw a punch or pulled the trigger.

Most of the time.

He thought about the deputy he had chatted with on his way into the building at the start of his shift. He wondered if her shell-shocked expression was a result of being run off the road or if the tight lines around her eyes were the aftereffects of the incident splashed all over the news. It was probably a combination of the two.

Harrison knew what it was like to have personal business laid out for public consumption. That was a big part of why he had taken a job with the sheriff's department in Quail Hollow. He never thought the small-town sheriff's department would be dealing with a case of excessive force. But he supposed people were people and bad decisions could happen anywhere. He had come here to get his head on straight and he hoped he could keep his distance from any interoffice drama. He wanted to do his job and go home at night with a clear conscience.

Such as it was. He carried a lot of guilt with him regardless.

As Harrison pulled out of the back lot of the sheriff's department, he noticed Deputy Spoth standing next to her personal vehicle. The petite blonde had caught his eye more than once, and not because she had arrived in a tow truck at the end of her shift this morning. And not simply because she was a woman—he had worked with plenty of female law-enforcement officers before. He noticed her because she seemed different. Almost too meek to do this job. Too nice. Yet she had somehow broken up a fight on the side of the road that, by all accounts, could have led to the death of a young Amish man. That was how he had interpreted the reports. Mumblings suggested other deputies thought differently. Not that he was willing to get involved in a heated debate.

Didn't concern him anyway.

Harrison didn't envy Deputy Spoth's position. Not all law-enforcement officers could understand how a fellow officer could testify against them. Some would silently support their fellow officer no matter what.

One side was right. One was wrong. Clear lines.

He had done that with his brother. Harrison had only seen his side of things. Had let his brother know of his disapproval under no uncertain terms. Had purposely alienated his brother in hopes that he'd realize the error of his ways. Had seemed like a good idea.

Everything had always been clearly black-and-white—until life served him up some bleak gray.

Harrison squeezed the steering wheel and shifted his focus to the female deputy standing by the open driver's side door. She had her hands planted on her hips and a frustrated expression on her face. At first he thought she was still carrying the weight of her rough shift in her posture until he dropped his gaze to the two flat tires on her personal vehicle.

He pulled up alongside where she was parked,

jammed the gear into Park and climbed out, allowing the engine and the AC to run. The deputy glanced up at him with an unreadable expression on her face.

"What's going on here?" he asked.

The woman held out her hand toward her car. "Someone slashed all four tires." Her cheeks filled with air, then she huffed in frustration. "Apparently, the number of people I've managed to irk has grown."

Harrison crouched down and ran his finger along the clean slice in the rubber. "Man…" He angled his head toward the row of patrol cars across the parking lot. The heat was pulsing off the blacktop surface and he could feel the sweat forming under his uniform shirt. "I can put a call in to a local garage."

"I already did. They're on their way." She dropped down on the curb and rested her arms on her knees, letting her hands hang limply. "Looks like bad things really do come in threes."

He narrowed his gaze, not sure what she meant.

"Patrol car towed in. Flat tires." She ticked the items off on her fingers. "Got suspended."

"Suspended? Why?" He thought she had come out smelling like a rose after her testimony against the other officer.

"New video." She didn't need to elaborate; her participation in the most talked about case was well known. "Apparently enough to make them question my involvement."

"Really?" He ran a hand across his chin, reminding him that he should have shaved this morning. "How so?"

"The video's not clear-cut, but a person with something to gain could suggest I used my baton on Elijah

Lapp." She shook her head, clearly dejected. "That's exactly what Deputy Reich's lawyer is doing. He's using the video to spread the blame. It's a mess."

"Who sent the video in?"

"Good old anonymous." She closed her eyes briefly and drew in a long breath, before finally meeting his gaze. "And now I'm out of a job."

She pushed to her feet and pulled out her cell phone from her duty belt. She walked around to the back of the vehicle and snapped a photo. "Don't let me hold you up. Pretty sure it won't do you much good to hang out with me."

He walked around to where she was standing to see what had caught her attention. He raised his eyebrows, surprised she seemed so calm. *Is fattgange* was written in soap on her back window. Gibberish as far as he could tell.

"What does that say? Anything?"

"It's Pennsylvania Dutch. You know, the language the Amish speak."

He hitched a shoulder. He had been here for less than a year, but other than a few bits and pieces here and there, he mostly heard the Amish speaking English, perhaps with a touch of an accent. "What's it mean?"

"Go away." Her tone was flat.

"I'm just trying to help." Harrison held up his palms and took a step back, not sure what he had said to offend her.

For the first time, the young woman's mouth curved into a grin and she laughed, adding to his confusion. "No, that's what *is fattgange* means. Go away. In Pennsylvania Dutch."

Harrison scratched his head and couldn't help but

laugh at himself. "Sorry, I haven't picked up much Pennsylvania Dutch yet, beyond the basics."

"You'll learn a little here and there, but most of the adults speak English. That is, when they want to talk to you. The Amish, as a rule, don't care to deal with law enforcement. The only problem you might run into is with little kids. Most of them don't learn English until they start school. But it's not likely you'll run into an Amish child without one of their parents or older siblings around."

Harrison nodded. "Yes, they mentioned that in my training." What little training the small-town sheriff's department had provided. He frowned. "You think an Amish person vandalized your car?"

"I don't know what to think. The car has been parked here all night on the edge of the parking lot by the trees. Pretty easy for someone to sneak in and out without being seen." She ran a hand across the top of her head. Her long blond hair had been braided, then pinned over her head, almost like the Swiss Miss girl. Something told him she was holding back, as if she had her suspicions as to who had vandalized her car.

"Go inside and report this. I'll wait. Give you a ride home."

"Are you sure?" Skepticism flickered in her eyes as she glanced toward the sheriff's station, then at him.

"Yes, go." He reached into his wallet and pulled out his business card and handed it to her. "My cell phone number's on here. If you come out and I'm not here, call me. I'll swing by and pick you up." He had no idea how long the report would take.

She took the card and slipped it into her back pocket. Harrison watched the deputy cross the parking lot

to the station. He sensed, rather than saw, another patrol car approaching. He tugged open his patrol car
door and the cold air from the AC hit his legs. The car
inched past, coming awfully close to his open door,
and stopped. Harrison squinted, unable to see the officer's face due to the brim of his hat.

The window slid down. Harrison tilted his head to
see inside. The officer had his wrist casually slung on
top of the steering wheel, blocking the name tag on his
chest. Dark sunglasses hid his eyes.

"A little advice for the new guy."

Harrison wondered how long he had to be here before he was no longer the new guy. He gestured toward the driver to get on with it even though he didn't
want his advice.

"Stay away from the chick. She's toxic."

Harrison crossed his arms and glared at the deputy,
struggling to place him, then finally remembering his
name: Colin. Colin Reich. Ned's son. No wonder he
had it in for Deputy Spoth.

"Thanks for the tip." Harrison's tone was even. He
had seen office politics take down the best of them.
He had no plans to stir the pot. A noncommittal answer was best.

Behind the wheel, Colin saluted him in a mocking gesture, as if he suspected Harrison was going to
do his own thing regardless. The man wasn't wrong.

"Don't say I didn't warn you," the deputy muttered
before closing the window and driving away.

THREE

"Where do you live?" Harrison asked Becky as he put the patrol car into Drive.

"Out on Asbury Road past the Millers' farm."

He cut her a sideways glance. "Mind telling the new guy where the Miller farm is?" Before she had a chance to answer, he lifted his hand in resignation. The locals often gave directions by landmark and if he didn't want to be forever known as the new guy, he had better figure it out. "Why don't you just holler when I need to make a turn? Sound good?" He gestured with his chin toward the road. "A left out of here?"

"Yeah." Her tone sounded as flat as the four tires on her car still awaiting the tow truck in the parking lot. A part of him wondered if whoever was taking their frustration out on her was doing it not just because she testified against another deputy, but because she was a woman. Despite the calendar year, a lot of guys still believed in the good old boys' club.

Harrison drummed his fingers on the top of the steering wheel as he slowed to look both ways before he pulled out of the parking lot and onto the road. "Everything go okay when you reported the incident?" The sheriff seemed like a pretty solid guy, determined to make a strong showing in his new position.

"Yeah, I guess."

His gut told him not to ask, not to get involved. But he couldn't help himself. "What does that mean?"

"Apparently, I've attracted some unwanted attention, including getting run off the road this morning."

This kind of behavior really ticked him off. Negligent drivers. Probably out drinking.

"The sheriff wanted to dismiss it as reckless driving on some back country roads, but now this…" She lifted her shoulders and let them drop. "Here, turn at the next road. It's quicker." She tugged on her seat belt and continued on about the sheriff. "If he hadn't already suspended me, he probably would have after my car was vandalized. I'm attracting the wrong kind of attention. The sheriff would probably claim a few more days off would be for my own good. Department morale seems at a low."

"Does the sheriff think it's someone in his department?" He scrubbed a hand across his face.

"Not that he'd ever say. But I wouldn't put it past Reich himself. He's a loose cannon." Becky ran the palms of her hands up and down the thighs of her uniform pants.

"His son works here, too." Harrison thought back to the officer who drove by slowly, warning him to avoid Becky.

"Doesn't help. All the other deputies will feel more loyalty to the Reich family than to me, unfortunately."

"You going to be okay?" He stared straight ahead as fields of corn whipped by on either side of them.

"Yeah." What else could she say? She wasn't exactly going to pour her heart out to him. He was a stranger.

"You need to hire a lawyer," he said matter-of-factly.

She shifted in her seat to partially face him. "You really think so? Isn't that expensive?"

"It might be too costly *not* to hire a lawyer. You need someone looking out for your best interests." He wished he had seen that his brother had got the help that he had needed instead of allowing his anger and embarrassment to put a rift between the two of them. "The sheriff's department has had a publicity nightmare after the beating incident. The video from your dash cam made it onto all the news stations from Buffalo to Cleveland. If this new video gets out, depending on what's on it, this story is going to grow legs and find its way into all the news cycles again. The sheriff's department will do anything to get out of the spotlight, even if that means throwing you under the bus."

"You can't be serious." She swept her hand across her mouth and eyed him wearily. "This is a small-town sheriff's department, not some big city."

"Office politics are office politics."

"But I didn't do anything wrong."

"Does the latest video support that statement?" His gut told him she couldn't be violent, but in an altercation, you never knew. Adrenaline and fear did things to people.

"Yes… I used the baton to separate the men." Becky tugged on the strap of her seat belt. "Reich's lawyer gave the sheriff a video of me approaching the men with my baton raised." She cleared her throat. "The rest of what happened is unclear. Whoever recorded it took off running, but…" She paused, rubbing her temples vigorously as if reliving the moment. "I used the baton to brace Reich and pull him off the kid. I didn't hit anybody. I mean, if I hurt anyone with the baton, it would be when I forced it against Reich." She blinked a few times. "I can't believe this mess. I only became a deputy because I wanted to help people. Now everyone is going to think I've turned evil." Her turn of expression sounded odd.

"Take a deep breath." He wanted to reach out and touch her hand, but decided against it. "Hiring a lawyer is a good idea, especially for the innocent." Well, for anyone. "Don't fight this alone. Reich has a lawyer," he added, if she needed more convincing.

"I don't know," Becky muttered. Before he had a chance to respond, her cell phone chimed. She yanked the phone from her duty belt and checked the number. "I should get this."

Harrison listened to a one-sided conversation. Obviously, someone Becky knew personally was in distress.

He reached over and touched her arm and mouthed. "What's going on?"

"Hold on, Mag." She held the phone to her chest. "My sister wants me to stop over. She's concerned about a neighbor's dog. *Again.*"

"Where does she live?"

"It's okay. I don't want to impose on you any more than I already have."

"I don't mind. I haven't had any calls anyway."

"Um, okay." Then into the phone. "Hang tight. I'll be right there."

Becky directed Harrison toward a house nestled among a cluster of Amish homes. "Right up here. Park on the road along the cornfields. Better if they don't see the patrol car."

"Are you going to tell me what this is about?"

Becky scratched her head. "My sister. She's worried about a neighbor's dog that ran onto the property. It's been an ongoing concern. The dog is hungry and not well cared for. We've suspected abuse, but I've handled it unofficially, returning the dog to his owner after they promised they'd take better care of it." She frowned. "Obviously, that's not working."

"Wait." Harrison angled his head to look up toward the home. A buggy was parked by the barn. An Amish family obviously lived here. "Your sister?"

"*Yah*, my sister." A twinkle lit her eyes. He had a feeling the amplified Amish inflection was for his benefit.

"Oh…" It was his turn to sound confused. "You grew up Amish?"

She pointed to her nose and said, "Ding. Ding. Ding."

"Oh… Do you want me to wait here, then?" Harrison asked, suddenly feeling a little discombobulated. *Amish? Really?*

Becky hesitated for a moment. "That would probably be best."

"Okay, I'll do that. I'll be right here." Now he was repeating himself, completely caught off guard by her revelation.

Becky climbed out of the patrol car and strode along the road and cut in between the cornfields, as if to go in undetected. He had read somewhere that the Amish shunned those who left their ranks. Perhaps Becky was sneaking in because she wasn't welcomed.

Harrison rubbed the back of his neck, replaying in his mind all the events that had transpired since he had held the door at the station open for Becky this morning. He hadn't had much interaction with the deputy since he'd moved here less than a year ago, but he would have never guessed former Amish worked as deputies. Were there others?

Now the warning in Pennsylvania Dutch to "go away" made a little more sense. But how a woman went from Amish to sheriff's deputy was beyond him. Maybe it was time he finally learned a little more about the Amish. And maybe Becky was just the person to teach him.

Becky strode up the dirt path between the cornfield and the neighbor's property. She undid the buttons on her cuffs and rolled up her sleeves, hoping to look a little less official in her sheriff's uniform. It was early enough that perhaps her parents would be too busy with chores to notice their wayward daughter had snuck in to meet with her younger sister out back by the shed.

She hoped.

But if she did run into them, she wanted to downplay the fact that not only had she jumped the fence, but she had also joined the sheriff's department. Her parents didn't need to voice their displeasure. It was a given, not that either of them had even discussed it directly with her. It was kind of hard to confront someone when you didn't talk to them.

When Becky got to the shed without being discovered, she heaved a sigh of relief. She didn't think her day could get any worse.

Until it had.

Mag—short for Magdaline—was sitting with her back pressed against the shed, a mangy dog in her lap. At seventeen, Mag was the youngest of the Spoth family children. Three brothers separated the bookend sisters, two of which were already married. Only Abram and Mag still lived at home.

"Hi, Mag." Becky crouched down and her heart dropped when she saw the pain in her sister's eyes. Becky gingerly touched the dog's matted hair. An unpleasant aroma wafted off the unwashed dog in the summer morning heat. Becky had to stifle a groan. "This poor dog found his way over here again, didn't he?"

Mag nodded, her lower lip trembling, making her appear much younger than her seventeen years and reminding Becky of the preteen she had left behind almost six years ago when she decided the Amish life wasn't for her. But now Mag was straddling childhood and the woman she would soon become. Would she choose to be baptized Amish or break their parents' hearts as Becky had done? Mag was a big part of the reason Becky chose to stay in Quail Hollow. Sure, she left the Amish, but she couldn't abandon her sister completely. Her three brothers had each other. Mag had no one.

Becky inspected the dog; open sores covered the pads of his paws. "He needs medical care."

"I know." Mag sniffed. "Are you going to make me return him, like last time?"

Becky looked toward her childhood home. She didn't see any sign of her parents. "*Dat* and *Mem* would want you to return him. He's not ours." Even as she made the argument, she wasn't convinced, especially since the owner had obviously ignored her warning to take care of his pets.

"But he's just a little puppy," Mag said, her words trembling as she fought back tears.

"No one can treat an animal like this. There are laws against it." Rage thrummed through Becky's ears as she grew more convinced that she couldn't hand over this dog to their neighbors. Not again. "Let's go talk to the Kings." The culmination of a few very bad weeks had suddenly reinforced Becky's spine with steel. At this exact moment, she didn't care about the consequences, not if it meant protecting this puppy.

"*Dat* won't like that." Mag suddenly had cold feet despite her fierce need to protect the dog. "I'll get in trouble for being disobedient." Their father had told Mag to stop meddling in their neighbor's business the last time the dog had wandered over. Becky heard the story secondhand when the sisters met in town for a quick cup of coffee. Their father wouldn't have liked that, either, but he had never expressly forbidden it.

"I'll take the blame. There's nothing they can do to me," Becky said. A look of admiration crossed her sister's delicate features, something Becky both cherished and dreaded. She didn't want to be a negative influence on her sister. Their parents also worried about her influence. Becky wasn't welcome at her childhood home. Shoving the thought aside, she held out her hand and helped her sister up. "Let's go."

Magdaline walked alongside Becky, holding the dog in her arms, the fabric of her long dress swishing around her legs as she rushed to keep up.

Becky slowed and held out her arms. "Hand me

the dog. I'll confront Paul. You don't have to get in trouble."

Paul King, the owner of the farm next door, and Becky weren't strangers. Far from it. But with their vastly different lifestyles now, they easily could have been. Not so long ago, he had driven her home in his courting wagon more times than she could count from Sunday singings. He confidently laid out the plans for their future, while silently she made plans for her own.

Their more recent exchanges had been over this very same dog. Paul obviously wasn't caring for the animals on his farm. Perhaps since his father had died and Paul had become the sole man of the house, he had let things slide. However, this time she wouldn't hand over the dog and leave. She wanted to see for herself what was going on at her neighbor's farm.

"It's okay, I'll take the dog over and talk to him," Becky repeated.

Mag held the dog closer, reluctant to let him go.

"Mag, I don't have all day." The sun rising higher in the sky was making her sweat in her deputy uniform. "Give me the dog and I'll handle the situation."

Mag lowered her eyes to the puppy nestled in her arms. "But if he takes the dog back, he won't be cared for. Even dogs are God's creatures."

A sense of pride filled Becky. Her sister had far more spunk than she had at that age. However, she feared that kind of grit would get an Amish *youngie* in trouble more often than not.

Becky tugged on the hem of her untucked uniform shirt. She'd hate to see what she looked like after the day she'd already had.

And it was still early.

Becky touched her sister's sleeve. "The truth is, since the dog belongs to Paul, it's very possible that we'll have to give him back. But there are laws against inhumane treatment of animals. I can…"

Her suspension. What could she really do while suspended?

"We'll figure this out. But first, I need to see what's going on next door. Give me the dog." She smiled encouragingly. "Go home. I don't want you to get in trouble with *Dat*."

Mag jutted out her chin and pressed her lips together, the picture of defiance. "No, I'll go with you. I'll get back before *Dat* and *Mem* find out I'm gone."

A little twinge of guilt zipped through Becky. She didn't mean to encourage her sister to disobey her parents, but deep in her heart, she couldn't imagine her parents would want to let the treatment of this dog to continue unchecked. Animal cruelty was the only way this dog could have sores on his body and matted fur. "Let's hurry up, then, so you can get back to your chores."

"Okay." Her sister seemed to cheer up a bit. Big sister to the rescue.

Becky hoped she didn't look as ruffled as she felt, but she wanted to make a serious impression on Paul. He needed to take better care of his animals. Maybe the threat of interference from law enforcement would make him fall in line, but somehow she doubted it. He'd seemed unfazed the last couple times she stopped over. The sheriff's department walked a very fine line when it came to dealing with the Amish. They wanted to respect their right to live separately while making sure laws were followed.

Becky followed the small path that led through a crop of trees to the Kings' house. Memories of a life lived so long ago came floating back. Memories she'd rather forget because they made her nostalgic. As a teenager, she used to run along this path to visit her friend Amy. And later when she started dating her friend's older brother, Paul, back when she thought her life would be like her *mem*'s and all the female ancestors before her.

Now, Paul, and his wife, Mary Elizabeth, owned the farm, his mother living with them in the *dawdy haus*. Paul's brother Amos still lived there, too, but was rumored to be getting married soon. And her friend Amy had married an Amish boy and moved across town like a good Amish girl. Actually, Amy's husband was the cousin of Elijah Lapp, the Amish boy who had been beaten by Deputy Reich. Elijah had ditched his car in front of Amy's house in hopes of taking cover in their barn, or so the gossip went.

Such was life in a small town.

Becky shook away all the memories pelting her as she came to a clearing on the Kings' property. She slowed and turned to look for her sister, who had fallen behind. The dog seemed content curled up in Mag's arms despite being jostled as she ran to catch up.

When they reached the barn, Becky held up her hand. "Wait here while I look inside. I'm not going to hand the dog over this time without seeing the living conditions." Most Amish kept their pets outdoors.

Becky pulled open the door and slipped through the small opening. It took her eyes a few minutes to adjust to the shadows. The smell of hay and manure, although unpleasant, wasn't unfamiliar. She was grateful she was no longer responsible for mucking out the stalls. A little pang of guilt poked her because she had left her sister and brother behind to do her chores.

The guilt ebbed away as curiosity took hold. From the far end of the barn, she heard mewling sounds, as if a small animal or animals were in pain. Blinking, her eyes adjusted to the darkness.

Something moved in the shadows.

She pulled her flashlight from her belt and directed its beam toward the heartbreaking sound. The eyes of at least a dozen dogs in a small cage glowed under the light. She reeled back on her heels with a gasp.

"What are you doing in here?"

Becky spun around. Paul lifted his hand to block the light that hit his hardened expression under the wide brim of his straw hat. He gritted his teeth. "Get that out of my eyes, woman."

Instinctively, Becky lowered her hand, but didn't turn off the flashlight. Paul had a short fuse when things didn't go his way. She remembered the sinking feeling she had as they discussed something regarding their future and his anger when she disagreed. He had fully expected her to be subservient as his wife. And why not? They both had grown up with similar role models in their homes.

Becky didn't see that for her future. She had her own ideas. And from somewhere deep within, she had mustered the courage to leave. Sometimes she wondered how.

Resisting the urge to shine the beam back into his eyes to make a point, she gestured toward the door. "Come with me."

She strode past him into the bright sunlight and

around to the back where Mag was standing out of sight. "Why is this dog—any of those dogs—not being cared for?"

Some of the bluster disappeared as his mouth worked, but no words came. The uncertainty in his eyes made her believe that he didn't know what to say. Perhaps he actually felt shame for the condition of the dogs.

"You didn't answer my question. Why are you here?" Paul tried to regain the upper hand.

Surprisingly, Mag spoke up. "Your dog wandered over to my farm again. He came through the woods." She spoke so softly she was difficult to hear above the dogs that had started barking in earnest at the commotion.

"This one keeps escaping." Paul reached out to grab the dog from Mag's arms. Mag pulled away and gave him her back, obviously determined not to relinquish the dog.

"I see stubbornness runs in the Spoth family." Paul huffed and crossed his arms. "Give me my dog. You said yourself it came from my property." It didn't seem to register with him that this was the very same dog they had previously returned on two separate occasions. How many dogs did he have in that cage? How had this one been fortunate enough to escape on more than one occasion?

A look of terror—of realization—crossed her sister's eyes and she took off running down the driveway, the awkward gait of someone holding on to something dearly as her gown slapped at her skinny legs.

"Mag!" Becky called out to her. She shared a brief

exchange with Paul and an idea hit her. "I'm not going to hand over the dog like last time."

Paul smirked, as if her threat was meaningless. "I think you have enough trouble not to go borrowing more." His hard-edged stare made her speechless. "I read the papers. What are you going to do, beat me up?" He laughed, the sound scraping across her nerves. He held out his hand as if to touch her, and Becky stepped back, out of his reach. "You must be scrappier than I thought."

Rage roiled in her gut, helping her find her voice. "Let me buy the dog," Becky offered.

"What are you talking about?" Paul said, growing angrier. "Just leave. That's what you wanted from the beginning, to leave the Amish, so don't come back here in your uniform and try to tell me what to do. You have no say over me. You, of all people, should know that." Paul strode down the driveway toward her sister. "She better give me that dog."

Protective instincts kicking in, Becky rushed after Paul. "You will *not* take that dog from my sister. Do you hear me?"

Paul spun around and glared at her. Seizing the moment, she reached into her pocket and pulled out the two twenties she had stuffed in there before the start of her shift last night, before her world was once again upended. She never knew when cash would come in handy, for lunch, for someone down on his luck, or for offering her former boyfriend forty bucks for his dog.

"I'm buying the dog." She jammed the money in his direction. "Isn't that why you have so many dogs in a cage? To sell them? I'm buying this one." That had to be the reason. The sheriff's department had answered complaints regarding suspected puppy mills among the Amish, but she had never come across one. Mostly, she had hoped the reports were false. How could a kind and gentle people be anything but loving toward God's creatures?

With a sour expression on his face, Paul swiped the money out of her hand. "Keep the dog. Now, get out of here."

Becky stared at Paul for a long moment, as if trying to decide her next move. She didn't have too many options legally right now because of her suspension, but he didn't know that. Maybe the threat of intervention by the sheriff's department was enough for him to clean up his act.

"Take care of those dogs. They need a clean, warm place to stay." Becky pointed to the barn. "Someone will be out to inspect the animals in the next day or two."

A muscle jumped in Paul's jaw. "What did I ever do to you?" Like always, he tried to turn things around. Cast the blame elsewhere.

"Take care of those dogs," she repeated, not bothering to soften the hard edge of her tone. The sun beat down on her, making her sweat. Becky hustled to catch up with her sister at the end of the driveway. Once there, she touched her sister's shoulder. She could feel her trembling. "Come on, sweetie. The dog is ours."

"Really?" Mag lifted her watery eyes. "But, what's *Mem* and *Dat* going to say when I show up with a dog?"

"Don't worry." Easy for Becky to say when, in fact, Mag had a very good point.

Just then, she noticed Harrison's patrol car pulling

up on the side of the road. He must have been watching for them. He climbed out of the patrol car.

"Everything okay?" With a concerned look on his face, he gently petted the dog in her sister's arms, as if inspecting it for injuries. This tender gesture touched Becky's heart.

"Yes, it is for now." She shot him a "we'll talk about it later" look. Then she gently scooped the dog out of her sister's arms. "I'll take care of the dog. Once he's all better, maybe *Dat* and *Mem* will let you keep him. Okay?"

"Okay," Mag repeated quietly, not seeming so sure. Becky understood the feelings of helplessness and lack of control while on the cusp of adulthood, especially among the Amish.

"I promise I'll talk to our parents about the dog."

Mag looked up with wide eyes. "Might be hard if they're not willing to talk to you."

Becky ran a hand down the dog's matted fur. "One step at a time."

Becky turned to steal one last glance at the Kings' property. Paul had disappeared, but his wife, Mary Elizabeth, stood on the porch and stared at them, clutching something to her chest. A light breeze ruffled the Amish woman's long dress. A whisper of something—nostalgia, déjà vu, relief, maybe?—made Becky tremble as a vision of what most certainly would have been her future flashed before her eyes. But it wasn't her life. She had broken up with Paul. She had left the Amish, her family.

Yet, still, on this sweltering day, she couldn't help but feel shadows of her past stretching out to claim her.

FOUR

Harrison cracked the windows on the patrol car, but kept the AC cranked up. Their newest passenger needed a bath and Harrison needed a little fresh air, but it was too hot to forgo the AC all together.

Harrison remained quiet after Becky had climbed into his patrol car. They watched her sister until the blue fabric of her dress was no longer visible from the road. Becky seemed satisfied that she had arrived safely home.

It was then that Becky told him about the dogs in deplorable conditions in a cage in the barn. She had convinced him to take her home and to worry about the animals later. That she'd figure something out. He imagined she had had enough for one day and it was barely midmorning.

He agreed.

For now.

It wasn't until he got to the first intersection that he asked for directions to her house. Between cooing reassuringly to the dog on her lap, Becky pointed out where to turn. When they arrived at her house, she thanked him and got out.

Something about dropping her off without further comment didn't seem right. He climbed out of the patrol car and strolled toward the porch where she struggled to hold the dog and fish out her door key from a bag slung over her shoulder.

"Do you need a hand?"

She seemed to regard him for a minute, before handing off the dog. He held his breath as the poor dog, through no fault of his own, smelled like…he couldn't even put it into words.

He crouched down and set the dog on the porch. The dog seemed to know this was his chance and bounded down the stairs and across the yard. Becky turned around and made an exasperated sigh.

"Hold on, I'll get him." Harrison hustled down the steps and caught up with the dog when he thankfully slowed to sniff around a tree. "Come on, you. I don't think you realize what a good thing you've got going here," he muttered to the dog. "Anyone who takes in a mangy mutt like you has to have a good heart."

When he looked up, he was surprised to find Becky standing a few feet away watching him. A hint of a smile whispered across her lips. She blinked slowly, exhaustion settling in around her eyes. "Thanks. I'll have to call the vet and then see about getting a leash and supplies for my new friend. And a bath is in order, of course."

"Listen, I have to get back on patrol, but I'd be happy to stop by after work. I know your car's out of commission. I could drive you into town and pick up a few supplies for your new roommate."

Becky rubbed her lips together as if she had just put

on Chapstick. "I can't impose. You've already helped me out a ton today."

Harrison tilted his head. "I don't mind." He glanced around her house and property. She had a well-maintained Dutch colonial house with a large front porch set back among the trees on a wide stretch of property. "You're kinda stranded out here until you get new tires." He shrugged, trying to act casual. He wasn't sure why getting her to accept his offer of help felt like a challenge. A challenge he wasn't willing to lose. Becky was certainly not like the women he was used to dating. His ex-girlfriend was, well, the opposite of Becky, not that he was looking for a date. He supposed the need stemmed from his desire to help out a fellow officer while she was down and out.

That was all.

Something I should have done for my brother.

"You never realize how much you take your car for granted until you don't have one." She smoothed the matted fur on the dog's head. "I do need supplies for…" She bit her lower lip. "I really should come up with a name for this guy." The dog playfully chewed on her hand. Becky looked up and laughed. "Chewie?"

Harrison couldn't help but smile. He hadn't had a dog since he was a kid. Seemed like much simpler times. Back then his little brother had thought Spot was a good name for their dog who, for the record, didn't have any spots. "Okay, Chewie, why don't you and your owner get inside where it's cooler?" He put a hand on the small of her back and led her toward the house. "I'll be back at four. We can grab a bite to eat first."

"Okay, as long as it's not too much trouble." He sensed Becky was giving him every possible out, but he didn't want to take it. He didn't like what had happened in the parking lot at work. If someone had the nerve to vandalize her car within a hundred feet of the sheriff's department, what would they be willing to do at her isolated home?

Most men and women in law enforcement were good, honest, hardworking people, but it wasn't unheard of for someone—out of a sense of misplaced loyalty, perhaps—to go after another person if they felt they had betrayed their own.

He wondered if this was the case now. Was someone getting back at Becky for testifying against a fellow officer? Or did this have to do with something else from her past? Harrison didn't know her at all to make the determination. But he hoped he'd let her get close enough to find out.

"Running errands with you is no trouble at all," he said as he glanced around her cozy house after she opened the door and they stepped into the small foyer. He hadn't made the time to decorate his place, unless you counted a couch and a large-screen TV as decor. He took a step toward the door. "I better get back on patrol. Lock up."

Becky paused and looked up at him. Something swept across her gaze that he read as a mix of confusion and perhaps a touch of fear. "Do you think that whoever nearly ran me off the road this morning or sabotaged my car would come to my home? I have no idea if the incidences are related, but I want to believe it's someone blowing off steam. Right? Not someone with real malice." Perhaps sensing the wistfulness of her words, she shifted to a more somber tone. "Ned Reich has been a deputy for a long time and he *does* have a lot of friends. Do you think they're trying to get back at me for ruining his career?"

"You didn't ruin his career. He's responsible for that."

Becky shrugged and wrapped her arms around her middle.

"It doesn't feel right to me." He debated how much to tell her, but at the same time, he reminded himself that he was talking to another law-enforcement officer, not a poor damsel in distress. He needed to be up-front with her. "It could be someone loyal to Ned. Maybe even his son. But you've had some negative press lately, too. So that extends the suspect pool. And if this new video is as bad as you say it is, it might lead to other people trying to take matters into their own hands. For all we know, this video could be going viral on the internet."

All the color seemed to drain from Becky's face. She touched her hand to her forehead. "Like a friend of Elijah Lapp's?"

"Perhaps. It's too early to tell." Standing in the small foyer, he tapped the decorative finial on the railing post with his closed fist. "You need to be careful."

"You're right. I will be." She pressed her hand to her duty belt as if she was checking for her gun that wasn't there.

"They took your gun?"

"And my badge." But he had a feeling she was more concerned about her gun right now.

"Do you have other firearms in your house?"

Becky jerked her head back. "You really think I'm going to have to shoot someone?"

Harrison rubbed his jaw. "I don't know what's going

on here. But a weapon might help you sleep better at night."

She bent down and touched Chewie's head. "I'll sleep better once the truth comes out. I had nothing to do with the young man's injuries."

Harrison nodded and reached for the door handle, making a mental note that she had never told him if she had a personal weapon. "I'll pick you up after my shift."

Later that day, while Becky excused herself to wash her hands, Harrison stared out the front window of the diner overlooking the sidewalk in the center of town. It was one of those rare summer days in Western New York that could give cities south of the Mason Dixon a run for their money. Many families—both Amish and *Englisch*, as he learned he was called—were out in full force, despite the heat rolling off the cement.

He supposed it beat a foot of snow.

The charm of Quail Hollow was growing on him, but he doubted he'd stay here, or anywhere, for the long haul. When he took this job, he took it because he needed an out. An out from Buffalo. An out from everyone who was checking in on him. An out of his own head where all his mistakes replayed on a constant loop.

But so far, he had only managed to get away from his hometown and his well-meaning friends. His nagging thoughts and guilt, not so much.

His cell phone buzzed. Normally he'd ignore it since he was off duty, but he had set a few things in motion today that he wanted to follow up on. "Deputy James," he said after accepting the call.

"Yeah, Harrison, it's Timmy. I took a drive out to the Kings' farm."

"How'd it go?" Timmy Welsh, besides being a deputy, was assigned to animal control, a tricky job in a town where most of the animal owners didn't want anything to do with law enforcement.

"Conditions were pretty bad. The sheriff told me to give Paul King a written warning. Tell him to clean up his act. I threw in a few threats on my own accord. Told him I'd be back and not to be surprised if I took the animals. Most Amish don't want to run afoul of the law. That usually does the trick."

"Thanks, I appreciate it."

"Sure thing."

Harrison ended the call, figuring Becky would be pleased with the latest developments.

He turned toward the voices. Becky was chatting easily with the waitress at the counter. Since he had dropped Becky home early this morning after work— her last shift for a while—she had undone her braids and gathered her hair into a long ponytail. It hung down her back almost to her waist. He blinked away, realizing he was staring. It wasn't any of his business how long her hair was or how nice it looked.

Becky turned slowly and glanced at him as if sensing his appraisal. A small smile hooked the corners of her mouth. He acknowledged her with a quick nod and turned his attention to the plastic menu in front of him. Despite having been in town for a while, he had never sat down in the diner to eat. He preferred to cook at home. Or maybe he just preferred to not deal with people outside of work.

He was still trying to figure out what it was about this woman that made him break all his rules.

When Becky slid into the bench across from him and brought with her a clean scent, maybe cucumbers, maybe something else, he suspected he partially knew the reason he was inviting her to dinner, even if he wouldn't admit it to himself.

"Sorry," she said, "just wanted to say hello to Patty."

Harrison nodded, but didn't say anything. He had a close circle of friends back home, but he couldn't imagine what it would be like to grow up and live in the same small town his entire life, where *everyone* knew your story. Where you'd actually stop to catch up with the waitress at the diner. Where people knew that you grew up Amish and left to become a deputy. Where soon they'd learn you were suspended.

Didn't sound too appealing, actually. He had experienced his own version of that in Buffalo after his brother died. It was a relief to go someplace where people didn't feel sorry for you.

Harrison opened his mouth to ask her what it was like to grow up Amish, but he found himself dropping his attention to an image of sunny-side-up eggs on his menu. He didn't like when people pried into his past and he should give her the same consideration.

Becky tapped the edge of the menu on the surface of the table. "Have you decided what you're having? The burgers are good."

Harrison set the menu down. "Then a burger it is."

"Oh, make sure you save room for dessert. They have the greatest shoo-fly pie."

"Just by the name alone, I know it's good."

Becky's eyes flared wide. "You've never had shoo-fly pie? How long have you been in town?" She didn't wait for an answer. "Oh, you're in for a treat." Her animated expression surprised him. She seemed so quiet, reserved, when in uniform. "A few different Amish families provide pies to the diner. When I was old enough to take the horse and wagon myself, I used to come in here and sell pies. Gave me some pocket money for when I decided to become a rebel." Her eyes flashed with excitement at the memory.

Harrison had a hard time imagining a bonnet covering her pretty hair. He had so many questions about the Amish, but he suspected those were questions for a second or maybe third date. His words skidded in his mind as if on a bullet train and someone flipped the brakes.

Easy boy, this wasn't a date. First, second, third or otherwise.

Oblivious to the commentary running through his head, Becky leaned forward and pulled a piece of paper out of her back pocket. "I have a list of things I need for Chewie. They should have most of them here in town." She smoothed out the wrinkled paper on the table.

"No regrets?"

Her brows snapped together, then smoothed. "About taking Chewie?"

He raised his eyebrows.

Becky waved her hand. "I didn't have much choice. The sweet dog needed a home. I have one. And the vet said she'd make a house call tomorrow."

Harrison liked her way of thinking, but in his world, few things were straightforward. "We can grab those things, sure. Shouldn't be a problem. By the way, I got a call from Deputy Welsh while you were washing your hands." She furrowed her brow, so he continued. "He works animal control. He stopped by the Kings' house and gave Paul a written warning. Said he'd be back to check in on the dogs."

"That's good." She bit her lower lip. "But I don't imagine Paul thought so."

By the way she referred to the owner of the property, Harrison suspected she had a personal relationship with the Kings. Of course she did; she grew up on the farm next door. He wanted to ask her how being former Amish impacted her job. In some areas, it must help, in others, they must look at her as a traitor.

Just then the bells clacked against the glass door of the diner. A shadow of concern crossed Becky's features. Harrison shifted in his seat to glance behind him to whatever had caught her attention. Two uniformed deputies strolled into the diner. Harrison recognized one as Colin Reich, the son of the suspended officer and the man who had warned him to steer clear of Becky.

Harrison gave them a subtle nod. "Evening, deputies."

Young Reich had his thumb looped through his belt as he sauntered past their table and glared at them. He must have signed on to work a double. He slid into the booth directly behind Becky. Her face grew red and the enthusiasm that was in her eyes when she was discussing her list of dog supplies had been replaced by something else. Fear? Regret?

The second deputy muttered a quick, "Hello," with a strained smile. The unspoken sympathy in his eyes suggested not all deputies were squarely behind Deputy Ned Reich, but refused to speak up. Harrison imagined there'd be a lot of tension within the sheriff's department until the beating incident of the young Amish man by a sheriff's deputy was just a speck in the rearview mirror of the town's collective memory. Unfortunately for Becky's future, memories were long and some incidents tended to forever stain a career.

Harrison reached out, falling short of touching Becky's hand resting on the table. He whispered, "We can go someplace else to eat, if you'd like."

Her gaze hardened and she whispered, "I didn't do anything wrong. I'm not going to run away with my tail between my legs."

From their adjacent table, Deputy Colin Reich made a disparaging remark about Becky. Harrison started to slide out of the booth. He wasn't exactly sure what he was going to do. A fist to the throat came to mind, but doubted that would do anyone any good, least of all, Deputy Reich. Before he had a chance to add his name to the suspension roster, Becky touched his hand gently. Her pointed glare stopped him in his tracks.

"Let it go. It's not important."

"How are you so calm about all this?" he said in a hushed whisper.

"How's it going to look if I'm involved in another altercation?" She shook her head. "Nope, I'm going to have to have faith that this is all going to work out."

She had far more faith than he had.

Becky unlocked the door to her home as Harrison lugged in the pet supplies. She raced to the mudroom and opened the door. Chewie was curled up on a temporary bed of blankets. He got up slowly and wandered over to her, skepticism evident in his eyes.

Becky crouched down and gently patted his head. "Poor guy, still trying to figure out who to trust, huh?"

"Where do you want the supplies?" Harrison stood in the doorway to the mudroom.

Becky glanced over her shoulder. "The kitchen is fine, thanks. Put the things on the counter. I'll have to make room in the cabinets."

She heard Harrison set the items down, then sensed him hovering in the doorway again. "I don't know if it's a good idea for you to be out here alone," he said, his voice thick with concern.

Becky slowly stood and stretched her back. "I'm not alone. I have Chewie." The little dog barked up at him, as if to say, "Yep, she has me."

Harrison ran a hand across his mouth, obviously not pleased with her quip. "Why do I think he'd lick an intruder to death?"

Becky shrugged and crouched down and touched the dog's head. "We'll be fine, right, Chewie?"

Becky crossed her arms, suddenly feeling very tired. It had been an exceptionally long day. She usually slept for a few hours when she arrived home from the night shift, but today, she couldn't quiet her mind in order to rest. Only now that she was back home did she feel the full weight of her exhaustion. And strangely enough, she was grateful she didn't have to work tonight.

"I'll walk you out," she said.

Harrison studied her, apparently recognizing when he was being dismissed. He paused at the door. "Are you sure? I can stay and help you get Chewie cleaned up."

"No, the utility sink is in the mudroom. There's hardly room for me." She blinked away the grittiness of her contact lenses. "Thank you for offering. I do appreciate everything you've done."

"Okay." The hesitancy in his voice knotted the tangle of nerves in her belly. Did he really think she was in jeopardy in her own home?

"Don't worry. I'll lock up." She ran a hand down her ponytail and twisted it around her hand. It still felt strange after two decades of wearing her hair in a neat bun. Lifelong habits die hard. "I am a sheriff's deputy, after all. Well, I think I still am. I'm trained to handle the bad guy." The humor in her tone didn't ring true. She cleared her throat and forced a reassuring smile. "Really, I'm fine." She ushered him toward the front door.

"Okay, goodnight." He glanced over his shoulder as he stepped out onto the porch. "You have my number if you need anything."

She waved. "Yep." She had pinned his business card to the bulletin board in the mudroom before she changed out of her uniform earlier today.

Becky stood in the doorway and watched until Harrison drove away. She closed the door and turned the lock, not something she was in the habit of doing. She flopped down on the couch and Chewie jumped up next to her. She ran a hand down his matted fur and turned up her nose. "You really are a stinky guy, aren't you?"

Groaning because she couldn't put this off any longer, she pushed off the couch and grabbed the gentle pet shampoo from the counter and wandered over to the utility sink. What was she thinking? A hose outside would be much easier. And faster.

She tapped her fingers on her thigh and recalled the big metal tub stored in the shed. She stared at the little guy at her feet. "Okay, you win." She reached into the bag and pulled out the new collar and leash. "Come on. Let's get you cleaned up."

Outside, the evening sun was still hot. Perfect weather to wash a dog. She unhooked the hose from the stand by the porch and dragged it toward where Chewie was digging in the dirt next to the steps.

"You're going to be a handful, aren't you? Stay there, I'll be right back." Becky hooked his leash around the railing for good measure, then wandered to the shed. The strong smell of wood baking in the sun hit her when she threw open the doors. The metal tub she had considered using was filled with topsoil. "So much for that," she muttered to herself.

She shut the doors and crossed the yard. She unwound the leash from the porch railing and led Chewie away from the steps. She didn't want a mud puddle at her back door.

She blinked a few times as her contacts grew cloudy. "I should have put on my glasses before coming out here." She blinked a few more times, trying to clear her vision. She let out a long sigh, looking forward to her evening on the couch. Looking forward to cuddling up with her freshly washed dog.

She held Chewie by his new collar and soaked him with the hose. She reached over for the shampoo and struggled with the cap. She let go of his collar and twisted the lid and took a whiff of shampoo. "This will make you smell like a new doggy." Becky laughed at herself. In only a few hours, she had become one of those people who talked to dogs. She figured it was okay as long as he didn't answer.

With two hands, she lathered up Chewie's fur. He

seemed to be enjoying himself. After he was nice and soapy, she adjusted the attachment on the hose while blinking against her compromised vision.

Ugh, these contacts.

She pressed the sprayer and a sharp stream of water hit the earth near Chewie's head, spraying some dirt. The puppy startled and with a yelp, ran toward the edge of her property bordered by woods.

Becky dropped the hose and started after him. "It's okay. I won't hurt you. Come on, Chewie."

She swiped the back of a soapy hand under her nose. A sharp pine needle scratched the underside of her foot. "Oww," she muttered to herself. *That's what I get for wearing flip-flops out here.*

Blinking rapidly, she slowed, fearing she was chasing her skittish dog deeper into the woods. "Chewie, come on, buddy," she called in her best "I'll never hurt you" voice.

Leaves crunched in the shadowed depths of the woods indicating steps heavier than Chewie's. During the fall, hunters often encroached on or near her property. But it wasn't hunting season. Maybe someone was hiking nearby.

Yet, she found herself frozen in place, listening hard against the competing sound of her roaring pulse in her ears. Her gut told her to run. Get inside. Lock the door. Her heart told her she couldn't let Chewie get lost in the woods. The poor dog had been through enough.

Pushing past her fear, she called again to her dog. "Come on, Chewie. Want a treat?"

With the offer of a treat, a little wet ball of fur came bounding out from behind a bush. "There you are!" The rush of relief made her eyes water.

She bent down to scoop him up when a crack sounded over her head. All her training kicked in. Adrenaline zinging through her veins, she gripped Chewie tighter and pivoted toward the house. Staying low, she bolted up the porch steps, praying that if they took a second shot, their aim would be equally bad as their first one.

FIVE

Becky slammed the mudroom door and turned the dead bolt and pressed herself flat against the wall. Her chest heaved as Chewie's wet fur soaked through her T-shirt. "You're okay," she cooed into her puppy's ear. No one was getting in. They were safe. Since she was a female sheriff's deputy living alone, she had taken precautions to secure her home with solid locks and an alarm system. But until now, she had never felt the inclination to use them.

She set the trembling dog down on the tile floor. He excitedly jumped at the door, his claws clacking as they left smeared prints wherever they touched, including her shirt. His incessant yapping did nothing to settle her frayed nerves.

Standing off to one side of the door, Becky pulled back a corner of the curtain and peered outside. She squinted into the heavily shadowed woods and couldn't decipher one tree trunk from the next or determine if, in fact, the shooter still lay in wait. She blinked again, frustrated with her contacts.

Yap. Yap. Yap.

She reached down and distractedly petted Chewie's head. "It's okay. It's okay. Shhhh…"

Yap. Yap. Yap.

She strained to hear above the noise of the dog and her racing heart. Were those more shots fired in the distance?

She glanced out again. Still nothing. Nothing that she could see. She bit her lower lip, debating what she should do. She wasn't helpless. She was a sheriff's deputy.

Who was suspended.

Without a gun.

Grumbling her frustration, Becky grabbed her cell phone from on top of the dryer and dialed 91 before pausing with her thumb hovering over the last 1. The harsh expression on the face of Deputy Colin Reich, the son of the officer she had testified against, came back to haunt her from earlier at the diner. In her heart, she knew most of her fellow deputies were good men and women, but someone obviously had it out for her.

Who could she trust?

Did she dare call dispatch to send a random deputy to help her? Would they?

Her gaze drifted to Harrison's business card tacked to the bulletin board over the washer. She stared at it for a second. She hated to bother him, but what choice did she have?

The crack of distant gunfire sounded above Chewie's incessant barking. She bolted upstairs and to her bedroom window, careful not to make herself a target. The tree branches swayed, playing tricks on her tired eyes. She ran to the bathroom and popped out her contacts and slid on her glasses. She returned to the window, still unable to see anything out of the ordinary.

More shots. They sounded far off. Not like the one that pinged off the bark near her head. She swallowed hard. What was going on?

With trembling fingers, she dialed Harrison's number and lifted the phone to her ear.

"Harrison." He picked up on the second ring, a coolness to his voice. She didn't take offense because of course, he didn't know who was calling.

Becky made a quick decision to play it cool. "It's Becky Spoth. Sorry to bother you," she rushed on, before he had a chance to say anything, "but something's come up." She hustled back down the stairs while she was talking. She opened the door to the mudroom and Chewie jumped up on her leg and barked frantically as if to say, "Don't ever leave me alone again." She patted his head reassuringly, trying to quell his barking.

"What's wrong?" Concern laced Harrison's voice.

"Hold on. Chewie's being loud. Let me see if I can get him to quiet down." She sat on the floor of the mudroom and pulled Chewie into her lap, ignoring the smell of wet dog and mud. He nuzzled into her damp shirt and settled in, his tiny, wet body quivering. "I was outside trying to wash the dog and a shot ricocheted off a tree near my head."

"Where are you now?"

"In the mudroom." She cleared her voice, not wanting to sound helpless. "I still hear shots, but they're farther away."

"I'll be right over. Stay inside. Away from the windows. Hold tight."

Becky ended the call. Chewie licked her chin. She

gave him a cuddle, glad for the company. "You're the cutest dog ever, but boy, do you stink." She ran her hand across the back of his sudsy fur.

Tilting her head up, she could only see the tops of the trees through the window. Pushing off the floor, she stood while Chewie danced around her feet, probably figuring they were headed outside again. "Not yet, buddy. Not yet. Let's see if we can finish your bath in the meantime."

After double-checking the lock on the door, she ran the water in the utility sink next to the washer until it turned warm. "Okay, let's get you cleaned up." Becky lifted the squirming dog into the large sink and held his collar while she sprayed him and washed the shampoo out of his fur. She shut off the water and Chewie shook his entire body, showering Becky and her glasses with droplets of water.

She couldn't help but laugh. She grabbed a towel from on top of the dryer and rubbed his fur while she had him contained in the sink. She plucked him out of the tub and set him on the floor. "Good as new."

Becky cut a glance toward the door and wondered what was taking Harrison so long.

Harrison grabbed his keys from the counter and ran out the door of the nondescript one-story house he rented on the edge of town. The real estate agent said it was within walking distance to schools and when she realized he was single, suggested it was a perfect fixer-upper. He wasn't in the market for either. He just needed a place to lay his head between shifts at work and this place was good enough.

Harrison sped to Becky's house. Once he arrived,

he did a quick jog around the perimeter—all appeared secure—when he heard shots in the distance. It sounded like they were coming from the south. Running toward his truck, he hopped in and called Becky. "Everything okay?"

"Yeah, are you here?"

"I am. But hold tight. I'm going to check the property behind yours. I heard shots in that direction."

Becky assured him she was fine, so he raced off to the quiet country road that ran parallel to her road. He slowed and pressed the button on the arm of his door. The automatic window whirred down. Crickets and birds chirping filled the gaps between the silence. Clouds of insects came to life as the sun settled on the horizon. He cruised slowly, searching the fields for any signs of people or cars.

A shot rang out.

His heart jackhammered as he pressed the accelerator. About a quarter mile up, he found some young men in a field. The ones who noticed him pull up in his personal vehicle seemed disinterested, which thrilled Harrison because that meant he probably wouldn't have to give chase. He wasn't in the mood. His hand brushed his personal weapon he kept in a holster under his shirt as he climbed out of the vehicle.

Then, on second thought, he pulled the gun out and held it down by his thigh. He'd want to react quickly if things went south. Someone obviously had a gun. His sneakers sank into the soft soil as he strode across the field toward the men. The earthy smell reached his nose, a mix of rich soil and dried vegetation.

As he got closer, he heard laughing. Males. Late teens. Early twenties. One was holding a rifle at his shoulder aiming it at a row of bottles set up on an old, run-down Amish buggy.

"Put the gun down!" Harrison called, planting his feet, ready to respond if need be, but man, he hoped he didn't have to. As far as he could tell, these good ol' boys were just having target practice.

The kid with the gun turned, still holding the gun up on his shoulder.

"Lower your weapon!" Harrison started to lift his.

The kid quickly laid the rifle down on the grass and held up his hands. "Easy man. We're just shooting some bottles."

Another kid, this one empty-handed, took a step back; a worried expression flickered across his face. "Who are you?"

"Deputy James." He scanned the faces of the four young men standing in front of him. It appeared that they only had one weapon and it was on the ground. "Any weapons besides that one?"

"No," one of the guys mumbled.

"Do any of you own this property?"

"No, we're just using it for target practice. No one cares," a second answered, not bothering to hide his annoyance.

"Why here?" The proximity to Becky's place unnerved him.

The same young man shrugged. "Someone suggested it. It's just some field. We ain't hurting anybody."

Harrison pulled out his wallet and quickly displayed his identification before stuffing it back into his pocket. "I had a report of shots fired." Better leave it vague.

He didn't want one of these guys harassing Becky. *If* they already hadn't. "Are all you guys good shots?"

"What's that supposed to mean?" One of the teens seemed to take great offense, as if Harrison had questioned his right to carry a man-card.

"Anyone decide to take a few shots out in the woods? Maybe have a shot get away from you?"

Another guy came forward, ready to complain when Harrison held up his hand. "Let me see your identification."

"What the...?" But they all got out their wallets and Harrison took a snapshot of all their licenses. It wasn't exactly protocol, but since Harrison was off duty and no one complained, he figured he'd get away with it.

Harrison pointed at the teen who had the gun when he arrived. "You have a permit?"

"Yeah." Another young man pulled out a piece of paper and showed it to him.

"Okay." Harrison kept an eye on the guy with the rifle until he had it safely packed away. As they turned to leave, Harrison added, "I don't want you guys using this land for target practice anymore." He lifted his phone to suggest he had their names and addresses if he wanted to cause them trouble.

He waited until they piled into an older model pickup truck, two guys hopping in the back. Then he turned toward the woods, trying to determine if he could see Becky's house from here. The dried leaves crunched under his muddy sneakers as he made his way through the trees. Something caught his attention in his peripheral vision. Adrenaline surged through his veins. He slowed his pace. There shouldn't be anyone there, right? He had already found the source of gunshots.

Something felt off. Or maybe it had just been a long day. He swatted at a cloud of tiny insects swirling around his sweaty head. He squinted into the dense woods as the evening light faded.

Nothing.

Maybe it was deer. A fox. Anything could be out here.

He kept trudging forward, pushing aside sharp branches and stepping over fallen trees, until he reached what he suspected was Becky's house. It wasn't until he got around the front that he knew for sure. Before he had a chance to knock, an incessant barking sounded on the other side of the door.

A curtain fluttered at the picture window overlooking the porch. A second later he heard the locks on the front door. Becky's concerned face appeared in the crack before she pulled the door open wide. Chewie ran out and jumped on his leg. He crouched down and petted the dog. "Nice guard dog, here."

"If I hadn't bent over to grab this little guy, I'm afraid you wouldn't be talking to me right now." The memory of the bullet zinging past her head and striking the tree sent renewed terror skittering down her spine. God had been watching over her today more than once, that was for sure.

Becky straightened and stepped back into the entryway, studying her front yard and the road beyond that. She really was isolated out here, but she loved her house. Loved her independence.

She just didn't love feeling vulnerable.

"Come on in," she said to Harrison.

He paused and looked down. She followed his gaze to his mud-caked shoes. He kicked them off before stepping inside.

"Did you find anyone?" she asked, trying to read the serious expression on his handsome face. A five-o'-clock shadow darkened his jaw, making her wonder what he'd look like with a full beard, not that she was interested in a man with a beard. She could have stayed Amish for that.

"I discovered some guys conducting target practice in the fields on the other side of the woods behind your house."

"That explains the muddy shoes." She sat down on the couch and patted the cushion next to hers.

Chewie hopped up on the couch, did a little circle and settled in next to her. She laughed and dragged a hand down his almost dry fur. "That wasn't meant for you. But good thing you're cute. And clean." Then to Harrison, "I think there's still room on the couch if you don't mind sitting on the other side of Chewie."

"Don't mind at all." When he sat, Chewie gave Harrison a quick, almost possessive glance, then settled his head down on his new master's thigh.

"Yeah, I cut through the woods from that field to your yard." He ruffled the dog's fur.

"What are you thinking? Someone was a bad shot?"

"I'm not sure what to think. I'll want to go out and see where the bullet hit the tree. See what it looks like. Maybe we can determine the make and model of gun. But first, I have something to show you." He leaned forward and pulled the cell phone out of his back pocket. "I asked them all for identification."

"They gave it to you? Even though you weren't in uniform?"

"I'm convincing that way." A small smile quirked the corners of his mouth. His imposing six-foot-plus frame probably had that effect on a lot of people. As a petite woman deputy, she had to work at commanding authority. Her meek upbringing in the Amish community did nothing to aid her there, either. She was proud of how assertive she had become, but like anything, she was a work in progress.

Harrison clicked a few buttons on his smartphone and held it out to her. "Take a look at their photos on their licenses. Take note of their names."

She took the phone from his hands. Their fingers brushed in the exchange and she caught his concerned gaze. She stared at the screen and didn't recognize the first guy, swiped her finger across the screen and looked at the next. Until she had scrolled through all four images.

"Do you recognize any of them?"

She twisted her lips and studied the screen. "Number one looks a little familiar. I probably saw him around town. Tyler Flint." She said the name out loud, as if it might jog her memory. She adjusted the screen to make the image bigger. *Neh.* She swiped to the next two photos. Jeremy and Todd weren't familiar, either.

Then she swiped to the last photo and studied it for a bit longer. "Lucas Handler looks a little crazed, but I wouldn't want anyone judging me by my driver's license photo. His name's not ringing any bells. None of them are." She handed him his phone. "What did they have to say?"

"They seemed annoyed that I was breaking up their fun."

"What's your sense? Do you believe it was an accident?" Chewie was perfectly content on the couch cushion between them, but Becky pulled the puppy into her lap and stroked the length of him, needing the distraction. How many near misses could she endure in one day and still delude herself by claiming it was "just an accident"?

Harrison sighed heavily. Not exactly encouraging. He reached over and rubbed Chewie's head playfully. "He cleans up nice."

"Yeah. I finished his bath in the sink in the mudroom after I realized it wasn't safe to go outside." She buried her nose in his fur and inhaled his clean scent. "He's much better." She picked up a paw and inspected it. "I think he'll be fine. I'll feel better once the vet stops over, though."

"He seems at home here."

Chewie's presence calmed her nerves. "I promised Mag she could have him if my parents agreed."

"Are you regularly in touch with your family?"

"How much do you know about the Amish?"

"Not much, but I'm learning." He straightened and held up his hands, perhaps thinking he had said too much. "I don't mean to pry."

"No, it's okay." She leaned back into the cushions of the couch and continued to stroke the dog's fur. It felt good to open up to someone. "I think the Amish invented tough love." She laughed quietly, but knew it didn't sound as breezy as she had intended. She always felt a little skittish when people asked about her past. Perhaps she felt like they were judging her.

Perhaps she was the harshest judge of all.

She drew in a deep breath and continued. "If I had been baptized, they would have shunned me. Basically ignored me and kept me separate until I realized the error of my ways."

"But you were never baptized?"

"No, not in the Amish faith, so technically, I'm not being shunned, but they do like to keep me at arm's length. They don't want me to be a bad influence on my sister." She shook her head. "I also have three brothers. Two are already married and Abram still lives at home, but apparently, they're mostly worried about Mag."

"I know it's none of my business, but wouldn't it be easier for you to leave Quail Hollow? Make a fresh start somewhere else?" he asked. The spark of curiosity in his warm brown eyes touched her. He sounded like he was a man who had perhaps run away from something himself.

"I don't want to abandon my sister. That's why she has my phone number to call me if she ever needs anything. My dad has a phone in the barn for his woodworking business. He makes end tables and such to supplement my family's income."

To say "my family" seemed disingenuous. Her father had turned his back on her the minute he had learned she had jumped the fence. Despite the heartache, she had made the right decision. She loved and respected her Amish family and neighbors, but she felt a calling beyond the life she would have been allowed to live as an Amish woman.

God had called her to another life.

Becky continued to run her hand down the length

of the dog, feeling like she had said too much. Harrison didn't need to hear all the details of her life. Simply put, she had left the Amish, but she hadn't allowed herself to leave Quail Hollow or her sister behind.

"Is that why you came to Quail Hollow?" she asked, needing to change the subject. "To get a fresh start?"

"Something like that," he said, his answer curt. Now she understood why he was reluctant to ask her questions. He hadn't wanted her to do the same.

"I guess I'm the one who's prying," she said, trying to lighten the mood.

When he smiled his entire face transformed. She almost didn't recognize him as the same serious man whom she saw around the station. "You're not prying. Just not much of a story to tell."

Somehow she doubted that, but let it drop.

Harrison pushed to his feet. "I want to take a closer look out back."

Together they went outside and found the bullet in the tree. He dug the slug out of the trunk with a pocketknife. Palming the bullet, he followed her to the back porch. The concerned look on his face sent prickles of unease washing over her skin.

"What is it?" she asked.

He gently took her by the arm and led her into the house and locked the mudroom door behind them.

Harrison pulled his gun out and set it on the kitchen island. "I'm not going to insult you and suggest you can't take care of yourself, but I'd feel better if you had a gun and I know you had to turn yours in when you were suspended. And you never answered me about having a personal weapon, so I'm assuming you don't…"

Her gaze drifted to the weapon then back to his face. He seemed to be looking right into her soul.

Becky swallowed hard. "You don't think the shot out back was an accident?"

He placed the bullet on the counter. "This didn't come from a rifle."

"I don't understand."

"The young men I talked to claimed they had only been shooting a rifle. If they had another gun, they didn't want me to see it."

Becky gripped the counter, feeling unsteady. Slashing tires as a warning was one thing, but firing a weapon in her direction? "Do you think they meant to scare me or kill me?" Her voice broke over the last two words.

"As far as I'm concerned, anyone who fires a weapon toward another human being has got to understand the risks."

"What do I do now?" Her breath came out shaky. "It all seems so hopeless."

"We need to take this information to the sheriff so the department can start an official investigation."

"What if this causes more problems for me?" Becky simply wanted to get her job back. Not be the focus of yet another investigation.

Harrison took a step closer to her. "You're not responsible for this. You can't blame yourself. You've done whatever you've needed to do." The intensity and concern in his voice unnerved her, almost as if it was personal to him.

"If I had kept my mouth shut…" She broke eye contact and studied the floor.

"You did the right thing. I won't let anything happen to you."

SIX

A short time later Harrison crossed Becky's dark front yard and reached out to shake Sheriff Landry's hand. "Thanks for coming out, Sheriff."

"Of course." Landry adjusted his belt on his blue jeans. Harrison's call had caught his boss when he was off duty, probably at home watching TV with his wife and two young children, judging by the family portrait on his credenza behind his desk. Some people actually had lives outside of work.

"Come in. Becky's inside." Harrison turned and led the sheriff into the house. Becky was standing inside the doorway, holding Chewie.

"Hello, Sheriff," she said, quietly. If her bloodshot eyes were any indication, all the recent events were wearing on the young deputy. "Let's talk at the island in the kitchen." She quickly met Harrison's gaze. They had left the bullet on the counter, evidence that the young men weren't telling the complete truth.

The three law-enforcement officers settled in around the island. Harrison explained the situation to his boss, who seemed taken aback. "You mean to tell me someone tried to shoot you?" His question sounded pointed, accusatory, almost, and Harrison wasn't sure why. Maybe he was reading too much into it.

"It seems that way, sir. If I hadn't bent down to pick up the dog, I'd hate to imagine…" Becky leaned over and set the dog down on the floor, perhaps to allow herself a moment to pull herself together.

The sheriff leaned back on his stool as far as he could without falling off and crossed his arms over his chest. "Why didn't you call the sheriff's department immediately?"

Becky's face grew flushed and she started to stammer before she paused and composed herself. "I had Deputy Harrison's number. I didn't want to make a big deal out of it if it turned out to be nothing."

The sheriff's gaze drifted to Harrison and then back to Becky. Was he trying to figure out their relationship? "I'm glad you reached out to me now."

Becky trailed a finger along the edge of the counter. Feeling the need to rescue her, Harrison spoke up. "I got identification from each of the men doing target practice."

The sheriff rubbed his jaw slowly, probably trying to determine if Harrison had followed procedure, but at this exact moment, Harrison didn't care. He placed his phone on the table and opened the photo app. He slowly scrolled through the photos, watching the sheriff's face. If he knew any of the young men, he wasn't letting on.

The sheriff scratched the side of his head roughly. "Send those photos to my email address. We'll start an official investigation." He planted his palms on the island and stood.

"Great," Harrison said, standing to join his boss.

"When I ran for sheriff, I campaigned on a platform of transparency." He seemed to puff out his chest. "I can't have my deputies running off on their own."

"I only called Harrison because I could trust him," Becky said. Her posture slumped and she blinked slowly as if realizing the implication of what she had said. Harrison wanted to reach out and squeeze her hand, reassure her, but he knew now was not the time or place.

The sheriff slowly turned to look at her. "Are you saying you don't trust the other deputies? Has anyone given you reason not to trust them?"

"I think Becky's afraid of backlash after testifying against Deputy Reich," Harrison said. "There's definitely been a coolness within the department toward her."

Becky held up her hand. "I can speak for myself." Harrison detected a hint of a tremble in her voice.

"Is that true?" The sheriff stared at her. "You think one of my deputies is out to get you?"

"I do feel like some of the officers wish I had kept my mouth shut. That's all." She fisted her hands and placed them in her lap. "I have a hard time believing one of them would hurt me."

"I'm glad to hear that." The sheriff sat back down and rested his elbow on the island, his posture more relaxed. "Let me assure you that anyone who harasses you will be dealt with severely." Sheriff Landry gave her a stiff smile showing all his teeth, reminiscent of his big face plastered on the billboard during the election. "I know this is hard for you, but you have to trust that the department will conduct a thorough investigation regarding the video."

"How long will it take?" Becky asked. "I'm eager to return to my job."

"I know you are," the sheriff said. "But there's more than one investigation to be done. I have to make sure we do this right."

"I didn't strike Elijah Lapp. I used the baton to break up the fight. To pull the two men apart."

The sheriff seemed to consider this for a moment. "Then our investigation will reveal that." He stared at her pointedly. "We have to allow the investigation to run its course. I know it's hard, but we have to do everything aboveboard. This way we can put this to bed once and for all."

Harrison recognized himself in the sheriff. Prior to his brother's death, he had been about rules, procedures and everything being black-and-white. But sometimes a strict adherence to rules meant compassion was lost. Meanwhile, real lives were being affected. Possibly ruined.

"Do you understand, Deputy?" the sheriff asked Becky, a hint of condescension in his tone.

"Yes."

"Good." The sheriff stood and adjusted his belt.

Harrison walked him to the door. "I can talk to the young men tomorrow." He wanted to see for himself why they didn't tell him about a second gun.

The sheriff slowed at the door and turned around. "I think it would be best if I have one of my more seasoned detectives follow up with that."

Harrison's head jerked back and he opened his mouth to protest when the sheriff held up his hand. "In an effort to be transparent—" there was that stupid word again "—I think it's important that someone not connected to the case conduct the interviews."

"What are you talking about?" Harrison glanced over his shoulder to make sure Becky was out of earshot. He was ready to plead his case.

"Trust me on this." The sheriff opened the door and left, leaving Harrison baffled.

"I suppose that went as well as expected." Harrison turned around. Becky stood in the doorway to the kitchen with Chewie in her arms. She stroked his back methodically.

"I suppose." Harrison replayed the conversation in his head. Something about this didn't feel right. It wasn't that he didn't agree with the sheriff that an official investigation should be conducted, he just hated being squeezed out of it.

"You need a lawyer." Sheriff Landry was going to protect his department no matter the cost. Becky had to look out for her own interests. If the sheriff was going to keep Harrison from helping Becky in an official capacity, he'd do whatever he could on a personal level.

"I don't know. Doesn't that make me look guilty?" She ran a hand down her long blond ponytail.

"You need to protect yourself."

"How does that work? I grew up Amish. We didn't use lawyers."

"You've told me before that the Amish don't care for law enforcement, either. Look at you now." He crossed the room and brushed his knuckles across the back of her arm, trying to encourage her. Reminding her that she was in a whole new world and had to play by new rules.

"How would I go about finding a lawyer?"

"I have a friend in Buffalo. I'd be happy to take you. He'll make sure your interests are protected. He'll fight for your job."

"Do you really think this is necessary?" After an extremely long day, Becky's skin looked ashen under the kitchen lighting.

"I have off the day after tomorrow. I'll see if I can get you an appointment then." Harrison tilted his head and forced her to meet his gaze. "I promise I'll be here for you every step of the way."

"Why would you do this for me?" Becky asked quietly, evidently still unsure. Her shoulders sagged in apparent defeat. Chewie lifted his head and licked her chin as if sensing she needed a little moral support.

Harrison needed for her to know this was far from over. That she had rights. That everything would work out. That she wasn't alone. A sadness whispered through him because he hadn't made this same show of support for his brother.

"I have my reasons," he said. "I hope you'll let me help you."

While sitting in the driver's seat, Becky flipped down the visor and stared in the mirror. She ran her finger along the darkened flesh under her eyes. "Ugh…" Another sleepless night, but at least she had her car back. The garage had returned it to her this morning with four new tires and detailing. Gone was the ominous warning in Pennsylvania Dutch to go away that had been scrawled on her back window.

That part of the vandalism puzzled her. Had a clever deputy known just enough Pennsylvania Dutch to threaten her and remind her of her place in society in one fell swoop? Or had someone from the Amish community really been harassing her? Friends of Elijah Lapp certainly had motive if they were following the press or the rumor mill, but she hated to think her Amish neighbors had run this far outside the law. Outside the *Ordnung*, the rules that the Amish district strictly followed.

Becky shoved the thought aside and jammed the key into the ignition and fired up the engine. She adjusted the AC to high and stuck out her lower lip and blew the wisps of hair that had escaped her ponytail from her face. Another sweltering day.

Fearing she'd go crazy if she spent another day cooped up in her house, Becky put the car in Reverse and backed out of the driveway. The vet had come to the house this morning and given Chewie some medication for the sores on his skin, but other than that, she said he was healthy. Now Becky's new companion was curled up on his cushy bed in the mudroom while she ran some errands. Errands that couldn't wait another day, especially if Harrison insisted she hire a lawyer.

Becky was a smart woman. She had made it this far in life on her own; she could certainly find a quicker way other than lawyers and lawsuits to put this mess behind her. She didn't do anything wrong and she wanted her job back. She couldn't shake the idea that lawyers were only for the guilty.

Mustering all the confidence she had, she drove to the farm near the sight of the brutal beating. She purposely waited until after the midday meal. If there was even a spark of hope that her old friend, Amy Miller, would talk to her, it would be if her husband John was out in the field.

Becky parked next to a cornfield, her car hidden from the house and the men working in the fields. The heat from the pavement blasted her cheeks. She plucked at her T-shirt, suddenly feeling underdressed. Nothing could make a former Amish woman more self-aware than showing up at an Amish home dressed in jeans and a T-shirt. Why hadn't she thought this through? Probably because as soon as the vet left, Becky wanted to leave, too. Before she lost her nerve.

As the gravel crunched under her sneakers, words like *humble* and *modest* from scripture pinged around her brain. Just because she had chosen to leave the Amish didn't mean she had chosen to disregard all of their teachings. She tugged on the hem of her T-shirt, pulling it down over the waistband of her jeans. She admired the Amish for their simple lives and their love of God; however, their way wasn't the only way to God. She wished their teachings allowed them to see that.

Becky pushed the swirling thoughts aside. Thoughts that always crowded in on her when she dealt directly with her Amish neighbors. Sometimes she did wonder if moving away from Quail Hollow would be easier than constantly confronting her past.

Taking a deep breath, she climbed the steps to the porch, and the slats creaked under her weight. The smell of something delicious wafted out through the open window. It made her nostalgic for home. Squaring her shoulders, she turned back toward the road and focused on why she was here: to find a witness to Elijah Lapp's beating. Someone to clear her name. She should have done this right away, but the sheriff had advised her against it.

From the porch, she searched the road. Other than

a fifty-foot clearing in front of the house, the scene of the altercation was obscured by the crops. Any witness would have had to walk to the end of the driveway. And from what she remembered from the chaotic scene, several people had. Tenting her hand over her eyes, she leaned back and stared up at the well-kept house, at the second-floor window. Her heart jackhammered when she saw an Amish woman staring down at her.

Amy.

Becky forced a smile and lifted her hand in a friendly greeting. She and Amy had grown up together and had been good friends until Becky decided to leave. Whereas Amy had followed the path set out for a young Amish woman: baptism, marriage and children.

Amy disappeared from the upstairs window and Becky waited, wondering if her former friend was going to come to the door. Becky scanned the landscape, holding her breath that John wouldn't appear and chase her away before she had a chance to talk to his wife.

Becky lifted her hand to knock, when the door flew open. Amy averted her gaze as if looking straight at Becky would somehow be breaking the rules.

"Hi, Amy."

Amy finally met Becky's gaze. "*Gut* afternoon. May I help you?" Becky should have been used to the stiffness and formality when it came to dealing with the Amish now that she was in law enforcement, but she and Amy had been the best of friends. Laughed together. Shared secrets together.

Perhaps Becky had made a mistake by not sharing the biggest secret of all. But that would have been an unfair burden to place on a friend. Neither Amy nor Mary, her two dearest friends, knew the plans Becky held in her heart.

Becky clasped her hands together, purposely trying to act meek, the opposite of what she had been trying to do since she left the Amish. She wanted her friend to see the girl she used to be, but jeans and a T-shirt certainly didn't help.

"Nice to see you," Becky said. "Can we talk?"

Amy's hesitant gaze drifted to the field. "I'm not sure what we have to talk about." Her words came out hard-edged.

"How is Elijah?" The young Amish man beaten at the side of the road was her husband's kin. Reports suggest he bailed out of his car at this location in hopes of taking refuge at his cousin's farm.

"He's recovering at home." Her tone suggested the unspoken words, "no thanks to you."

Becky wanted to ask if he talked about the incident, but she wanted to ease her way into the topic. And part of her was afraid of what he might have said.

"I was wondering if you could help me."

A crease of concern lined Amy's forehead below her white bonnet. "I don't see how I can."

"Were you home the afternoon Elijah was hurt?" It sounded more benign this way. Passive, as if there was no way she could have had an active hand in his injuries.

"*Yah*, I was home." Amy's eyes clouded over with an emotion Becky couldn't quite pinpoint.

"Did you see anything?" Becky twisted her clasped hands and her stomach knotted.

"*Neh*, I was settling the baby."

Shame heated Becky's cheeks. In another lifetime, she would have made a quilt for her friend's baby or at the very least, brought over food for the family. "Congratulations. I heard. A baby girl."

Amy nodded and a smile lit her face like it used to when they were girls and giggling over a shared story and lunch. "She looks just like John." She shook her head, a twinkle brightening her eyes. "Poor kid." But she didn't mean it. She was pleased that the child resembled her husband.

"I'm sure she's beautiful. Maybe I can see her sometime…" Becky left the question hanging, knowing that as long as she was an outsider and law enforcement, she wouldn't be welcomed into her friend's home. Not as a cherished friend. She cleared her throat, getting back to the topic at hand. "Did John see anything?"

A mask descended and Amy seemed to bristle. "Perhaps you should wait until he comes in from the field. You can talk to him yourself. Other people from the shcriff's department have been here, you know." She plucked at the folds of her skirt. "We want life to go back to the way it was, *yah*."

"The sheriff's department is trying to make sure justice is done." Becky's mind drifted to the chaotic events of that fateful afternoon. "I remember a lot of people watching. Did you know who was here?"

"*Neh*, the baby keeps me busy."

Was she hiding something?

"A video surfaced from that day and I was trying to figure out who took it."

Amy pinched her lips and shook her head again. "You're best to look for someone from your world.

It's doubtful the Amish would be taking videos. You know that."

Becky also knew that plenty of Amish, especially the *youngie*, bent the rules during their running around time. But she didn't want to press her friend. Bowing her head, she finally said, "I'm desperate. I need help. The sheriff's department thinks I hurt Elijah and I need to find witnesses to prove that I didn't. Otherwise, I could lose my job."

Amy's face brightened. "If you lost your job, would you come back?"

"Come back?"

"To the Amish. You could confess your sins to the bishop. I'm sure they'd welcome you back as long as you confessed." The hopefulness in her friend's tone broke Becky's heart. She missed her friends. But not enough to return. She wasn't sorry for leaving, so confessing in front of the Amish community, asking for forgiveness, would be a greater sin.

Becky gritted her teeth and stepped back. The wood slat on the porch let out a loud groan. She hadn't come here to confess. She wasn't interested in returning to the way of life she had run away from, but she needed to be careful not to offend her friend.

She needed friends, not that Amy would count herself among them.

"Thank you for thinking of me, Amy, but I'm happy with my life." Mostly. Becky threaded her fingers and finally worked up the nerve to ask the question she most feared the answer to. "Does Elijah remember what happened?"

Amy shook her head tightly. "I have not asked him."

She lifted her head with a steely gaze. "We want to move forward."

Becky opened her mouth to say something and a baby cried from somewhere in the house.

"I have to go."

"Okay…but if you hear anything, can you let me know?"

Amy stood with her mouth pressed into a grim line before saying, "To be in the world, but not of this world. You don't need to be trapped by the evils of the world." She reached for the door handle. "Perhaps you should think about returning to us. Our hearts are open to forgiveness."

A tenet of the Amish faith was forgiveness. Becky understood this because she grew up with it. Love your enemies. Leave vengeance in the hands of God. Whenever a tragedy struck the Amish community, their ability to readily forgive their transgressor often made the national news alongside the crime itself. Forgiveness was their duty.

Becky gave her friend a quick nod, acknowledging she had heard her, but she wasn't willing to comment. What could she say? Was her community ready to forgive her for leaving the Amish? Or did Amy think Becky needed forgiveness for hurting one of their own?

SEVEN

Later that day, Harrison parked his truck in Becky's driveway and crossed the yard to the front porch. The grass, dry from a long stretch of no rain, crunched under his footsteps. He had run home just long enough to change his clothes after his shift. He could have called Becky, checked on her over the phone, but if he was being honest with himself, he wanted to see her in person. Make sure she was doing all right. She seemed defeated after the visit from the sheriff last night. As if her chances of returning to work anytime soon were slim to none.

Harrison jogged up the steps and decided he'd act casual, pretend he wasn't genuinely concerned with her state of mind.

If only I had checked on my brother.

If only I had listened to my gut instead of my pride.

Harrison was determined to be there for Becky, but since they were simply working acquaintances, he'd have to be subtle. He could claim he was in the neighborhood. Tell her in person about the appointment he had set up with his lawyer friend in Buffalo.

He laughed to himself. No way was anyone ever "in the neighborhood" when you lived out in the sticks.

Harrison plucked at his shirt, wondering if this heat spell would snap anytime soon. He lifted his hand and did a quick little knock, sounding out a rhythm. *Really casual.* Deep within the house he heard Chewie barking. He turned and studied the road from the vantage point of the front porch. Heat rose from the pavement, but a nice breeze whispered through the leaves in the trees surrounding the property. It was peaceful out here. Quiet.

He turned back toward the house, listening for footsteps, something to indicate Becky was coming to the door. Nothing. A small knot formed in his gut.

Where is she?

Her car was in the shop. She couldn't be far. He jogged down the porch steps and walked around the property, hoping he'd find her outside even though he had warned her that staying inside was safer.

The sudden stillness made the fine hairs on the back of his neck stand on edge. He scanned the house and property. His attention stopped at the tree line, the heavy shadows mocking him. He wondered if the sheriff had made any progress in investigating the young men conducting target practice yesterday. Harrison had taken the liberty to use their identification to look up each of the men in the system. None of them had records. *Maybe* it had been an accident. Maybe one of them, for whatever reason, had been reluctant to produce the gun used during the wayward shot. Maybe that was the reason. Nothing more. *Who's going to admit to being reckless?* They could face charges.

Harrison climbed the two steps to the back door and knocked. Chewie barked wildly, his nails scraping against the door. Harrison cupped his hand on the glass on the back door and through the gauzy sheer curtain he could see the dog's tail wagging wildly. "Hey, buddy," Harrison said, "where's Becky?"

The interior door from the kitchen to the mudroom was closed. Had she gone out somewhere and put Chewie in the mudroom for safekeeping?

A new thought crept into his subconscious. He stepped away from the glass and took a deep breath.

He had gone to his brother's home under the guise of a wellness check. He pounded on the door. No answer.

Just like now.

Harrison tilted his head from side to side, trying to ease out the tightening between his shoulder blades.

He had been called out to Officer Sebastian James's home because everyone knew they were brothers. "Thought you'd want to know. He didn't show up for his shift," dispatch had told him in a somber tone as if they already suspected the worst.

Part of him wanted to tell her Seb wasn't his problem anymore. That once Seb chose drugs over job, over family, he was on his own. Harrison no longer wanted to hear the constant barrage of questions.

"How's Seb doing?"

"Glad to hear he got through rehab and got his job back. This drug epidemic is out of control. Sorry your brother got wrapped up in it. Looks like that's all behind him now."

Wrapped up in it? As if his brother hadn't slid that first needle into his arm. As if it wasn't a choice.

But his brother had sworn he was done with it. Drugs were in his past.

Harrison clenched his jaw as he jogged down the

porch steps and around to the front of the house, trying to dismiss the images that haunted him.

Seb, his little brother, slumped against the bathroom wall with a needle in his arm. His eyes staring absently at the pink tile of their childhood bathroom. Where Seb used to have to use a stool to reach the sink to brush his teeth.

The hot sun beat down on Harrison's head. He scratched his eyebrow and paced the gravel driveway, wishing Becky would answer the door.

How did anyone move past this kind of tragedy?

He let out a long, slow breath, trying to calm his rioting emotions. Everyone wanted to know why he left Buffalo to be a cop in Quail Hollow, some small town in the middle of nowhere.

This was why.

He thought distance would ease the pain. Make him forget. He suspected some of his friends knew the reasons, but he never talked about them. Working among the deputies in Quail Hollow who didn't know his backstory was easier than constantly seeing the sympathy in his fellow officers' eyes.

Harrison had come to a lot of conclusions since his brother's untimely death. People made choices, sometimes with disastrous consequences.

Some people stood by their family and friends no matter what. Harrison was ashamed to acknowledge he wasn't one of those people. Now he had to live with the guilt.

Life isn't black-and-white.

If he had listened to Seb when he first came to him. If he hadn't enacted tough love when it came to his brother, would he still be alive?

Harrison second-guessed himself every step of the way until he finally had to walk away from a job and a home he shared with his brother.

Until he found himself in Quail Hollow on the porch of a rookie deputy, worried that perhaps she had succumbed to the pressure. Found an escape.

That's Seb. Not Becky.

A trickle of sweat rolled down his forehead and a weight pressed on his chest. From the short time he had grown to know her, he sensed she had no one to rely on. As it was, she was straddling two worlds. Neither were welcoming.

Nothing would change until she cleared her name.

"Don't leap from point A to Z, buddy," he muttered to himself, realizing he was letting his past experiences get the best of him.

He strode to his truck for his cell phone. One quick call and he'd know where Becky was. Dilemma solved.

As he stood with the truck door open, he heard a car approaching. He hadn't realized he'd been holding his breath until the car slowed and turned into the driveway.

Becky.

She climbed out and angled her head, a look of surprise widening her eyes. "Did I forgot you were coming?"

"No, not at all." He was finally able to breathe. "I stopped by after my shift." He held out his hand, trying to act casual. "You got your car back."

Becky patted the roof. "Yes, they dropped it off this morning. Feels good to have wheels again."

"That's great." If he had known, he wouldn't have conjured up the worst-case scenario. Perhaps he had further to go in his recovery than he thought if his mind went spiraling out of control at the first sign of trouble.

The gravel crunched under her sneakers as she walked past him toward the front door. "Want to come in? Get something to drink? I can't believe how hot it is outside." Her cheeriness seemed forced.

Harrison followed her through the house and into the kitchen. She opened the mudroom door and Chewie leaped out as if sprung from prison. She playfully rubbed his head, then went to the fridge. "Iced tea?"

"Sounds great."

She filled two glasses and handed him one, seeming to study him with a watchful gaze. Then suddenly, she looked away and snatched the leash off the hook. Chewie ran over to her, eager to go outside. "I need to let the dog out."

Drink in hand, he followed her to the back porch. She let the lead out so the dog had a lot of space to wander without getting away. She leaned a hip on the railing. "I should consider getting a fence, if I'm going to keep Chewie. Or I suppose I should approach my parents to see if Mag can keep him."

"I sense you're reluctant to talk to your parents."

"That's a story for another day." She rested an elbow on the railing. "Is there a reason you stopped by?"

"I made an appointment with a lawyer in Buffalo for you."

She worked her lip and he fully expected her to refuse or at least be evasive, but she looked up at him with resolve in her eyes. "Okay."

Harrison scratched his jaw. "Why the change of heart?"

She laughed. "Didn't you tell me I needed a lawyer?"

"Yeah, but, I figured you'd push back."

Becky plopped down on the back steps and Chewie bounded over, nuzzling her thigh. Harrison sat on the step, one above hers.

Becky threaded the slack leash through her fingers. "I have to do something or I'll go stir-crazy here." She flicked him a quick glance over her shoulder, then turned her attention back to Chewie, who was sniffing around a tree trunk. "I stopped by the farm next to where Elijah Lapp was beaten."

Harrison clenched his jaw. "You shouldn't have…"

"My friend, my former friend, Amy Miller, lives there."

"I didn't realize that." Harrison watched her bend and twist the leash.

"I'm tired of waiting to get my job back. I had hoped Amy would vouch for my character. Perhaps she had witnessed the events of that day." There was a faraway quality to her voice. "She knows the real me. I'd never hurt anyone. But she's not going to help me. Her desire to stay separate and punish me for leaving the Amish is stronger than our friendship ever was." There was a brittleness to her voice.

"Perhaps she didn't see anything. Maybe you're reading too much into it." He tried to reassure her.

"She believes she's doing what she needs to do because they love me and want me to come back."

Hadn't Harrison felt the same way about his brother? *If he sees how angry I am, he'll stop. If he knows I won't be there for him, he'll make recovery stick.*

Becky absentmindedly fluffed the fur around Chewie's snout. "Unless I want to lose everything I worked for, I need to help myself. And if that means hiring a lawyer…"

She pushed off the steps and turned to face him, swiping the back of her shorts. "What time is the appointment?"

The next day, Becky met with the lawyer for forty-five minutes and his reassuring nature allowed some of the tension to ease from her shoulders. Maybe she wasn't alone in this. She had rights and this lawyer would fight for them. For the first time since Elijah ended up in the hospital, she felt like she had a plan. Felt like she was being proactive and not waiting for someone to make a decision on her behalf.

The lawyer opened his office door and Harrison quickly stood. He had used his day off to drive her to Buffalo and then sit patiently in the waiting room. He looked handsome in khaki pants and a navy golf shirt. She still couldn't figure out why he insisted on being so helpful, but she appreciated it.

"Everything okay?" he asked.

"It's good to know I'll have someone pushing for reinstatement on my behalf." Becky glanced at the lawyer.

"I'll do some digging and we'll get moving on this." The lawyer shook her hand, then Harrison's. "Meanwhile, you have my phone number if you need me, Deputy Spoth."

Becky drew in a deep breath. How strange that she had grown up on a small farm in Quail Hollow and now she had business in a law firm in a glass skyscraper in Buffalo. "Thank you."

As Harrison and Becky headed toward the elevator, he asked, "So, it went well?" He pushed the down button.

"Encouraging. Definitely." She smoothed the lapel of her business jacket.

"That's good. The sheriff's department has to understand you're going to fight for your job. I get the sense the sheriff doesn't want any problems and he might be dragging his feet on getting you reinstated. He's afraid of making the wrong decision, so he's not making any."

"That's a pretty strong assessment of him."

Harrison rocked back on his heels. "I'm good at reading people. He's new and he doesn't want to jeopardize his reputation. You've heard him going on and on about transparency." He shook his head. "He's into the politics of it all."

Becky took off her suit coat and draped it over her arm. "I just want my job back."

The elevator doors slid open and they stepped into the car. The smell of perfume from a recent passenger lingered in the small space. "My head tells me this is the right path, but a part of me worries I'm handling this all wrong. What if I'm building a wall between myself and the sheriff?" Hugging her jacket to her chest, she turned to face him. "Won't this make working for Sheriff Landry harder?"

"That's what they want you to believe. There's a procedure for these things. They know the rules and they're hoping you'll go it alone. Once they know you have representation, they won't play fast and loose with the rules."

"I thought I was a rule-follower." She had proved herself wrong when she left the Amish. The doors opened on the lobby floor. Prior to leaving the Amish, she often wondered what the inside of one of these fancy buildings looked like. Once when she was younger, their family had hired a driver and a van and had taken a rare trip to Niagara Falls. She was in awe of the world outside her own. Maybe that was when her curiosity began. A great, big world existed out there.

She often wondered if her parents regretted that trip. Regretted showing her a life outside of Quail Hollow.

As Harrison and Becky crossed the marble lobby, a few women dressed in business suits pushed through the glass revolving doors. Becky ran a hand down her jacket self-consciously, getting the sense that hers had been bargain basement while theirs probably cost more than a few of her paychecks. One of the women, carrying a coffee, strode confidently in their direction.

Again, Becky's mind drifted to all the lives she had never lived, could never imagine living. Was it easier or harder to find joy in life once you knew about all the opportunities in this great, big world? That was probably why the Amish shunned those who left.

Curiosity was contagious.

The woman seemed to take interest in Harrison and slowed down. She waved to the other women. "I'll see you back in the office." The woman's gaze then dropped to Becky, a small smirk tugging at the corners of her pink lips. "Harrison…" The intimate nature of the way she said his name caught Becky's attention.

"Hello, Courtney," he said. Was that a muscle twitching in his jaw?

Courtney tilted her head. "What brings you to my building?"

"Some business on the tenth floor."

"Legal trouble, huh? No lawyers in little ol' Quail Hollow?"

"The one I needed works here." He gently touched

Becky's arm. "This is Deputy Becky Spoth. Becky, this is an old friend of mine, Courtney Ballston."

Courtney extended her hand and Becky shook it. The woman's keen inspection made Becky feel like she was pressed between glass slides.

Feeling like she was intruding on a private moment, Becky greeted the woman, then turned to Harrison. "I'll meet you outside."

He handed her his truck keys. "I'll meet you in the truck."

"Okay." She took the keys, gave Courtney a polite smile and strode toward the door. The air was hot, but it felt good to be outside instead of in the sterile confines of the shiny marble lobby.

With the weight of the key fob in her hand, she strode toward the parking garage across the street. It still amazed her that structures existed for the sole purpose of parking cars.

She laughed to herself. Would she ever get used to the outside world? She pulled open the door to the stairwell and the smell of garbage and standing water assaulted her. Jogging up the steps to the second floor, she thought about her conversation with the lawyer. He had told her she had a few options regarding her job, and one included suing the department. He said he'd contact the sheriff's department and request a copy of the video. See if they could authenticate it. Apparently, videos could be edited to appear one way when things were actually another. Was that what had happened?

Becky couldn't remember every detail from the event because of the adrenaline coursing through her system, but she didn't strike Elijah. It wasn't in her nature. Maybe if someone had altered the video like the lawyer suggested, this could be all over. She'd get her job back.

What if that only proved the video was real? Apprehension sloshed in her gut, extinguishing her momentary flicker of hope. Since the entire event wasn't captured on video, she'd need to find a witness. And her friend Amy who lived near the incident wasn't talking.

Frustration weighing her down, Becky pushed open the stairwell door on level three. She had to blink to adjust to the heavily shadowed parking garage She should have paid more attention when they got out of the truck, but she had been following Harrison's lead while simultaneously trying to quiet her rioting nerves. She had never dealt with a lawyer before. And she hadn't anticipated having to locate the truck in the parking garage on her own.

Becky held out the key fob and pressed the lock button. The chirp of Harrison's truck echoed somewhere close by. She followed the memory of the sound to the next row over. She pressed the button again and saw the red brake lights flash.

Her heels—which she wasn't used to—clacked on the cement parking garage. The interior felt claustrophobic, especially to someone like Becky who had grown up on a farm.

A flush of dread she couldn't explain washed over her. She quickened her steps and checked over her shoulder. *No one.* But her imagination was full of all sorts of crazy notions.

It's just the stress.

When she reached the truck, she clicked the unlock button this time and heard a click-click. She reached for the door handle, when footsteps rushed toward her. Before she had a chance to react, a solid body slammed her into the side of the truck. Pain ripped through her hip and ribs.

She opened her mouth to scream, when a hand clamped over her mouth, making it impossible.

"You're dead," a deep voice growled.

As terror shot through her veins, the words of the bishop came flooding back, a cautionary warning she had refused to heed.

There is evil in the outside world. We must remain separate.

Becky should have listened. It was time for her to pay for her sins.

EIGHT

"New girlfriend?" Courtney asked after Becky pushed through the glass doors and disappeared across the street to the parking garage.

"Becky's a deputy in the Quail Hollow Sheriff's Department," Harrison said, wishing he and Becky had made it out of this building before Courtney had returned from lunch with her friends. He should have known better than to come here, but Declan Atwal was one of the best lawyers he knew, not to mention they were friends from law school.

Courtney's gaze drifted to the elevator. "And you brought her to your buddy Declan's office because she's in trouble." She sighed heavily. "I thought you went to Quail Hollow to get your head on straight." She lifted a perfectly groomed eyebrow, obviously suspicious of his motives. "Getting wrapped up in someone else's drama isn't going to help. You have to learn how to get out of your own way."

"Nice to see you, too, Courtney." Harrison didn't bother to hide the sarcasm in his tone. Their relationship had fractured even before his brother's death. But it was Seb's death that had sealed their fate. Harrison clung to the guilt that he had left his brother swinging in the wind. Whereas Courtney refused to live her life with any regrets and couldn't understand Harrison's. His brother had made his own choices and suffered the consequences, however dire. This clarity certainly made Courtney a fantastic litigator. She was a bulldog with a bone, never deviating from her mission. She had told him more than once, "You can't let your feelings get in the way."

"I'm worried about you. I thought I'd hear from you once you left Buffalo." The compassion she tried to force into her tone sounded more like condescension. He had been gone nearly a year and she hadn't bothered to call or text, either. "I expected even if you didn't want to stay in touch with me, you'd stay in touch with someone here. *No one* has heard from you."

"I'm fine. I've been busy. Don't worry about me." He hated that he sounded petty.

"I do worry about you." She leaned over and pushed her empty cup into the garbage can. The lid shut with a clatter as she pulled her hand away quickly. "We all do."

"I appreciate it. Well, nice seeing you."

He started to turn to leave when she reached out and brushed her fingers gently across the back of his hand. "You don't have to stay in exile. You could always come back. Practice at the law firm." Harrison had decided to become a police officer after a stint with the prosecutor's office. That had been a sticking point from the beginning with Courtney. She had always envisioned two professionals, dual incomes, two point five kids, *if* they had kids. Perhaps he hadn't been the one who had been fair. He shouldn't have changed the course of their lives midstream.

Or he should have been up-front about what he wanted in life from the beginning. He wanted to follow in his father's footsteps. He only had the courage to do that after his father's passing. But he could have never predicted the derailment of his life after his brother's death.

"Practicing law is not for me."

"You should give it another try," she said, exasperated. They had been through this many times before they officially broke up.

"That's not what I want to do. And you know it."

"You're not still blaming yourself for Seb's death. It wasn't your fault."

"I should have been there for him." He averted his gaze, not wanting to risk that all-too-familiar look of sympathy he always got. "Listen, I need to go." Becky had to be wondering where he was. He hadn't meant to keep her waiting this long.

"Oh yeah, I'm sure you don't want to keep your girlfriend waiting." Courtney's tone was drenched in sarcasm with a hint of jealousy. She always had a way of reading his mind—claimed she knew him better than he knew himself—but today he wasn't in the mood to engage.

"Nice seeing you, Courtney. You look good." She always did.

Courtney hesitated a moment, the look in her eyes suggesting she was calculating something, but then thought better of it. "I need to get back to work." She lifted her hand and wiggled her fingers at him. "Don't be a stranger."

He nodded and turned toward the exit. Why did he feel more like a stranger here now than he did in Quail Hollow? At least there he didn't have to pretend he was something he wasn't.

He pushed through the glass revolving doors, then jogged across the street toward the parking garage. When he opened the door to the stairs, a man dressed in black with a mask over his face burst through the door, narrowly avoiding a collision.

"Hey!" Harrison yelled, before his mind jumped to Becky. He gave a quick glance toward the fleeing man, then decided Becky was his first priority. He started up one flight of stairs before he heard squealing tires. He jumped out of the stairwell onto the second floor and just missed the taillights of his vehicle speeding down the ramp.

Had someone stolen his truck?

Or was Becky driving? Going after the guy dressed in black?

Harrison made a split-second decision. He spun around, reentered the stairwell and bolted down the stairs and burst out onto street level. He hoped that Becky was behind the wheel of his truck and not stuffed into the back under a tarp or—another horrible thought darted through his mind—sprawled unconscious on the hard concrete three stories up.

Pumping his arms, he reached the exit of the parking garage and found Becky yelling at the attendant to lift the tollgate or she was going to plow through it. Harrison flashed his badge and the baffled guy who didn't make enough money to deal with this kind of stress, entered his little glass building and the tollgate suddenly lifted.

Harrison jumped into the passenger seat and braced himself against the dash. "Care to tell me what's going on?"

"Did you see a guy dressed in black running away from the parking garage?" Becky leaned forward on the steering wheel, peering down the road, one way, then the other, her eyes wide. Her breath labored.

"Go to the right," Harrison suggested. "I saw him bolt out of the stairwell and take off toward the park."

The wheels on the truck squealed on the pavement. Becky gripped the steering wheel tightly, praying she didn't crash or run into a pedestrian. Flooring it on the country roads was one thing; here in the city was something altogether different.

Frustration rolled over her as they sped past parked cars and office workers returning from lunch. Her gaze darted all around her. "You see him?"

"No."

She slowed, realizing he could be anywhere. And it wasn't likely that he'd be running down the street with his mask on. It was sweltering out and besides, a knit ski mask would be like a neon sign blinking, *I'm guilty. I'm guilty.*

She pulled over and jammed the gear into Park. "He's gone."

"I'll put a call in. The local cops can investigate. The parking garage has to have cameras."

Harrison made a call and gave the local police a description.

Becky shifted in her seat, then ran a hand down her long ponytail. "I was walking to the car when that guy jumped me from behind."

Harrison ran his gaze down the length of her. "Are you okay?"

She waved her hand in dismissal. "He didn't know he was trying to mug a sheriff's deputy who had training in self-defense." She winced at the memory of his nose crunching under a swift blow with the heel of her hand. Direct hit. "A few strategically placed strikes and he took off." She shook her head in disgust. "I thought about going after him on foot, but I had on these stupid shoes. How do women even get around in these? My feet are killing me." The flow of words spilled out on a wave of adrenaline.

"You're okay? Are you sure?"

"Yes, of course." She tapped the center of the steering wheel with her fist. "I wish I'd caught the guy. He'll probably wait for the next victim in some dark parking garage. Creep."

"Becky…" Harrison seemed to be waiting for her full attention.

She turned to him. "What?"

"Did you ever consider that you were the target?"

She furrowed her brow. "Here? In Buffalo? I don't…" Her shoulders sagged and she plucked at her sweaty blouse. She once again remembered that trip to Niagara Falls as a young Amish girl and how her parents had warned her of the dangers. To always be vigilant. Evil lurked in the outside world. Wasn't that what this was about?

The ubiquitous evil the Amish talked about.

"No, he couldn't have been targeting me. Quail Hollow is a good hour's drive from here."

"We can't rule it out. Maybe someone followed us

here. If they attacked you in Buffalo, maybe they hoped it couldn't be traced to the events in Quail Hollow."

With the adrenaline subsiding, a sadness settled in her heart. "This is getting out of control." She needed air. She pushed open the truck door and stepped out onto the pavement.

"Where are you going?"

"I want you to drive home. I need to let my nerves settle."

Harrison climbed out of the passenger seat and met her around back. He took both of her hands in his and forced her to look into his eyes. "You're fine. You did great fending off your attacker. They'll think twice before coming after you again if it wasn't a random event."

They both knew it wasn't.

Becky swallowed hard and nodded. "Thanks. All my training has paid off." She just wished it didn't have to.

Back at her house, Becky leaned her hip against the kitchen center island and winced. She was a little sore from the attack, but grateful that was all she was. *Thank God.* She flipped open the lid of the Chinese take-out container. She peeked at the beef and broccoli and drew in a deep breath. "I've never had Chinese food. It smells wonderful."

Harrison unloaded the other little white boxes and plastic containers, taking a moment to bend down and pat Chewie's head. "You're not serious."

She lifted a shoulder in a half shrug. "They don't have a Chinese restaurant in Quail Hollow and I guess the times I've been away from here, there were so many other options to try."

He stared at her for a long minute as if he were looking through her. "I can't imagine what it was like growing up Amish."

A piece of broccoli fell off the spoon she was holding and plopped onto the counter. She picked it up and tossed it onto her plate. "Not much to imagine. What you see is what you get." She sat down on the other side of the island. She grimaced when her hand hit against the counter. She examined her fingers. The heel of her hand was already turning a shade of blue from where she made contact with her attacker.

Harrison sat down next to her with his plate. "Are you sure you're okay?"

"Yes, I'm fine. I can't say the same for the guy."

With his fork dangling over something that looked fried and wonderful, he said, "Tell me exactly what he said."

Becky wiped her napkin across her mouth and closed her eyes, recalling the feel of his sweaty hand on her mouth. His hot breath whispering across her ear. "You're dead."

Harrison pushed his rice around with his fork. "I hate to think someone from Quail Hollow followed us today. What did Sheriff Landry say when you called him?"

"I gave him all the details. He said he'd follow up here, but it was now an issue for the Buffalo Police Department." She shrugged. Before leaving Buffalo, they had filed a report at the station and had driven home in mostly silence. "I feel like the walls are closing in."

Harrison set down his plastic fork and reached

out and covered her hand. "I'm going to help you get through this."

She flinched. "I didn't do anything wrong, but I'm suffering the consequences." She slid her hand out from under his. "I'm the one without a job."

"Not for long."

"You don't know that," she said accusingly.

"You're taking all the right steps. You'll get your job back."

"The rules seem arbitrary." She picked up her fork and poked the branches of the broccoli. "I thought the hardest decision I'd ever have to make was behind me. Leaving the Amish was tough, but at least within their community, everyone knows the rules." She tilted her head. "A person might not like the rules. But everyone knows them." She lowered her voice. "Maybe I made a mistake by leaving." A knot formed in her stomach and she suddenly wasn't hungry anymore.

"Why did you leave?"

She looked up slowly, a bit surprised by his question. Most people wondered, she realized that, but most didn't ask.

"I felt like I was living a life that wasn't mine." She swallowed hard. "From the time I was a little girl, I'd look around the farm, at my mother, and wonder if this was all life had to offer." Heat suddenly swamped her face and she turned away. "Forgive me. I don't mean to disparage my mother. She's a good woman. But I'm not built like her. I never found satisfaction from cooking, cleaning and taking care of a husband." She shook her head. "Even now it makes me twitchy. I wanted to be on my own. There's a big world out there." She cut

"4 for 4" MINI-SURVEY

We are prepared to **REWARD** you with 2 FREE books and 2 FREE gifts for completing our MINI SURVEY!

FREE Value Over $20!

You'll get...

TWO FREE BOOKS & TWO FREE GIFTS

just for participating in our Mini Survey!

Dear Reader,

IT'S A FACT: if you answer 4 quick questions, we'll send you **4 FREE REWARDS!**

I'm not kidding you. As a leading publisher of women's fiction, we value your opinions... and your time. That's why we are prepared to **reward** you handsomely for completing our mini-survey. In fact, we have 4 Free Rewards for you, including 2 free books and 2 free gifts.

As you may have guessed, that's why our mini-survey is called **"4 for 4".** Answer 4 questions and get 4 Free Rewards. It's that simple!

Thank you for participating in our survey,

Pam Powers

To get your 4 FREE REWARDS:
Complete the survey below and return the insert today to receive 2 FREE BOOKS and 2 FREE GIFTS guaranteed!

"4 for 4" MINI-SURVEY

1 Is reading one of your favorite hobbies?
☐ YES   ☐ NO

2 Do you prefer to read instead of watch TV?
☐ YES   ☐ NO

3 Do you read newspapers and magazines?
☐ YES   ☐ NO

4 Do you enjoy trying new book series with FREE BOOKS?
☐ YES   ☐ NO

YES! I have completed the above Mini-Survey. Please send me my 4 FREE REWARDS (worth over $20 retail). I understand that I am under no obligation to buy anything, as explained on the back of this card.

☐ I prefer the regular-print edition
153/353 IDL GMYM

☐ I prefer the larger-print edition
107/307 IDL GMYM

FIRST NAME   LAST NAME

ADDRESS

APT.#   CITY

STATE/PROV.   ZIP/POSTAL CODE

him a sideways glance. "A big world out there," she repeated, "but I decided to stay in Quail Hollow."

"You don't have to defend your decision to me." He
spoke like he had experienced what it was like to live
a life that didn't feel like your own.

"I feel like I've had to defend my decision to
everyone—including myself—every day since I left."
She unwrapped a little bag and looked inside to find
a small roll. She didn't want to be rude and lift it to
her nose to smell it. "What is this?"

"A vegetable egg roll. Try it. If you don't like it,
I'll finish it." He smiled and her heart fluttered a bit.
She quickly lowered her gaze. When she had left the
Amish, she had vowed she'd forever be independent.
If she wasn't willing to be tied down to the Amish way
of life—which included marriage—why would she do
it outside when she was free?

Her hand fluttered around the hollow of her neck
and she wondered if freedom wasn't all that it was
cracked up to be. Maybe the reasons the Amish had so
many rules was to protect the people from themselves.
From all the worldly temptations.

She took a bite and set the roll down on her plate.
After she swallowed the mouthful, she said, "I thought
I'd be happier once I left the Amish."

Harrison leaned in close. "Don't mistake your current mood for how things are always going to be."

She slowly lifted her eyes to his. "You sound like
you're speaking from experience."

"Yeah, you met Courtney today. We were engaged."

"Oh." Becky wasn't sure why she suddenly got a
twinge of…was it envy?

"We met in law school. I never felt like I was where

I needed to be. I grew up the son of a police officer and always thought that wouldn't be enough. I worked for the prosecutor's office for a few years, but after my dad died, I decided to follow in his footsteps." A corner of his mouth curved into a smile. "Courtney called off our engagement because she wanted to be married to a lawyer. Not a cop. She thought my next stop should have included a fancy corner office."

Becky studied his face. "Are you happy being in law enforcement?"

"For the most part."

"For the most part," she repeated. "Does this have something to do with why you left Buffalo and came here?" Becky asked, feeling a bit like she was being nosy. Her mother would have scolded her to mind her manners, but Becky had always been inquisitive. It was why she was here and not content to marry Paul and live in the Amish way. She had felt the walls closing in on her when Paul expressed his interest. She was grateful—and amazed—that she had been strong enough to leave before their engagement was published.

"It's a long story." Harrison moved around a piece of white rice on his plate.

Becky leaned back and held up her hand. "I ask too many questions."

"I don't mind, but I don't want to bore you."

"I'm willing to listen," she said. She owed him that much after everything he had done for her since this mess started.

"Well, the short version is that after I left the prosecutor's office, I became a police officer. I had a strong sense of right and wrong while convicting the bad guys. Now I had a chance to work as a police officer, taking criminals off the street." He lowered his voice in frustration. "I wanted to get in there, get my hands dirty."

"Sounds admirable."

"It can be. But sometimes it takes more than determination. It takes compassion."

Becky scrunched up her nose. "For the bad guys?"

Harrison put down his fork and rubbed his temples as if something pained him. "Sometimes someone we think is the bad guy just doesn't see any other way out."

Harrison glanced up even though he wasn't sure he could look Becky in the eye. She seemed too trusting.

"What happened?" She reached over and placed her hand on his forearm.

"Shortly after I joined the police force, my mom got sick. She told me to keep an eye on my little brother, Seb. He was a rookie officer." Even now referring to his brother in the past tense was like a punch to the gut.

Becky brushed her thumb back and forth in a soothing gesture across his arm. He wondered if she even realized she was doing it. He had noticed her doing the same thing when she held Chewie.

Speaking of which...

Harrison glanced around to find the dog curled up, sleeping on his bed in the corner of the kitchen. A part of him hoped the dog would jump up and save him from spilling his guts. He didn't want Becky to start looking at him like his friends did back in Buffalo.

Poor Harrison. His brother overdosed. He found *him. Did you know that? It must have been awful. Needle still in his arm.*

He stared off into the distance and ran his palms up and down the thighs of his pants, trying to shake that last horrific image of his brother. Apparently sensing his distress, Becky said, "You don't have to talk about it. Not if you don't want to."

He found himself drawn to her compassion. "I do." He hadn't realized that until he said it out loud. Even though he had only grown to know her over the past few days, he wanted to share this part of his life with her. He felt a certain connection to her.

He no longer felt alone.

"My brother Sebastian got involved with illegal drugs after he got hurt on the job. A back injury led to painkillers led to heroin use."

To her credit, Becky kept her expression even. He had learned to anticipate judgment, as if a person who used drugs didn't deserve compassion.

He had been one of those people.

"When I discovered his drug use, I employed tough love. Told him to knock it off. Told him he was bringing shame to the family name."

"I'm sorry," Becky whispered, still offering a comforting touch to his arm.

"Instead of pushing him away, I should have been there for him."

"I'm sure you did your best."

"But I didn't. He died less than a week after returning to work. He had made it through rehab. He had been doing well. But I still acted cool toward him. I wanted to let him know he hadn't been forgiven. He had to work for it. That I had zero tolerance for his drug use." He ran a hand across his mouth. "Who did I think I was? I'm not perfect." He shook his head. "Maybe if he knew I was in his corner…"

"You didn't know…" Her voice trailed off.

"I should have known." A muscle ticked in his jaw. "I was the one who found him in the bathroom of our childhood home." He plowed a hand through his hair and he suddenly felt sick, just as he had done every time he remembered the pallid color of his brother's skin.

Becky didn't say anything; she just looked at him with that pained expression all his friends back in Buffalo gave him.

"I found a journal he kept in rehab. There were pages and pages about me and stuff we did as kids growing up and how he missed me and wished I would support him more."

Harrison sniffed and fought to hold the rest of his emotions at bay. "Seb made a huge mistake getting involved with drugs, but I didn't do anything to help him."

Becky cleared her throat softly. "We all do the best we can. You didn't know how this would end."

"I should have. As a police officer, I've seen it enough. But I was more worried about appearances. How his drug use reflected poorly on me. On our family. I was terrified of enabling. Like, if I relented, he'd think I was okay with it."

He pinched the bridge of his nose. "Biggest mistake of my life and unfortunately, there's no redo on this."

"You need to forgive yourself."

Harrison pushed the stool away from the kitchen island and carried his paper plate to the garbage can. He stepped on the foot pedal and the lid snapped open. He tossed his plate in, then turned back to her. "I don't know if I can ever forgive myself. I can't even bear to live in the house where he died. To run into our mutual friends. To see his old locker at the police station downtown." He rubbed his jaw. "I thought moving here would get me out of my head. But clearly it hasn't."

Becky set down her fork and stood. She approached him cautiously as if he might spook. He imagined how he looked standing there. "I'm sorry you had to go through all that. Perhaps you need to find faith to find peace."

He bit back a laugh, something that came automatically when people suggested things like prayer, faith— what did that mean anyway? "Faith? Where was God when Seb shot up on the bathroom floor?" He clenched his jaw to stop from spilling out all the arguments for why *faith* was not going to help anyone. Yet, as strongly as he felt, he didn't want to offend this sweet woman who was only trying to help.

"You didn't deserve that," he said quietly as he stepped around her. "How did you keep your faith after everything you've gone through? I mean, how can you not be resentful that your so-called God-fearing parents ignore you? What kind of hypocrisy is that?"

Becky radiated a calmness he didn't understand. "My parents are good people. They think that by giving me the cold shoulder, I will return to the Amish way. It is meant to be redemptive. They want me to come back into the fold." Becky tilted her head, forcing him to meet her gaze. "Just like you did what you thought you had to do for your brother."

Harrison groaned at the comparison.

"You could have never anticipated the outcome," Becky continued. "You thought Seb would make the right decision and give up drugs."

"I should have anticipated a relapse." Harrison wasn't ready to acquiesce to her argument.

Becky shook her head. "I'm not trying to compare drug use with running away from the Amish, but one thing we have in common are family issues. My family loves me and you loved your brother."

"I did."

"We all do the best we know how." She snapped closed the lid on a takeout container. "If you ever want to take me up on going to church, you know where to find me. I find it keeps me centered when everything around me is falling apart. I may have left the Amish, but my Christian faith is strongly intact."

Harrison slid the takeout container from her hand and leaned down and brushed a kiss across her cheek. Becky jerked back in surprise. Before she had a chance to respond, he said, "Thanks for being a friend. I haven't had many since moving to Quail Hollow."

"Anytime," she said breezily, clearly uncomfortable. He hated that he had made her feel that way. "Um, do you think you'll return to Buffalo?"

"I still own my parents' house. I suppose I could find another police job either in Buffalo or the surrounding communities." He shrugged. "I haven't given it much thought, but I also never thought Quail Hollow would be long-term. I needed to get away."

"I know that feeling." She took a step back and spun around and returned to the task of closing containers and snapping on lids to the Chinese takeout. "You know, it's me who should thank you. Without your introducing me to your lawyer friend and—" she lifted a container "—Chinese food, my life would be far drearier." She opened the fridge and started stuffing containers inside.

Becky's movements suddenly seemed manic as if she was trying to be cheery. It made Harrison wonder what he had said. Perhaps he had shared too much.

NINE

The next day, Becky sat on the couch with Chewie curled up by her side. She had the blinds drawn against the gorgeous sunny day. It was easier to pretend her life hadn't gone off in a ditch this way. She didn't have many friends as it was and certainly the ones she had in the sheriff's department thought she was toxic. Even Anne, her closest friend and assistant to the sheriff, hadn't returned her phone calls.

Her memories drifted back to the conversation she and Harrison shared last night over Chinese food. In a way, they were kindred spirits. Both struggling with life's circumstances and family issues. The one difference: Harrison was truly alone. All his family had since passed. Hers was on the other side of town, choosing to pretend she didn't exist.

All except Mag.

She wasn't sure which was worse.

TV remote in one hand, she flipped through the stations, getting tired of all the shows she didn't feel like watching.

After recent events, this was the only way she felt safe, cocooned in her house. Harrison had called her this morning to check in on her and she feigned cheeriness. She rambled off a long list of things she planned to do around the house that she never had time to do when she was working full-time. Yet, here she sat on the couch feeling too blah to move. She didn't want him to feel like he had to come by to check on her. He had already done too much. She shouldn't be depending on him. And she didn't want to be his "get over his guilt" project because he hadn't been there for his brother.

That's harsh. The man's genuinely concerned about you.

She turned up the sound on some all-hours news station to drown out the constant chatter in her head. Eventually, she began to doze. Her dreams were wild and disjointed. Stress did that.

Something startled her out of a dream—she might have been in pursuit of a speeding car or maybe she had been walking across a muddy field sinking up to her knees. Sitting up slowly and wiping the sleep from her eyes, she tuned in to a quiet knock on the door. Chewie, who had apparently also been sleeping next to her on the couch, lifted his head, looked at her, then looked at the door, then put his head back down. She couldn't help but laugh and patted him playfully on the head. "Some guard dog you'd make."

She squinted at the clock on the cable box and realized it was too early to be Harrison, unless he decided to stop by during his shift. Untucking her legs from under the blanket, she stood and shook out her right foot that had fallen asleep. Running a hand through her hair, she walked slowly toward the front window— Chewie in tow—and was surprised to find a horse and buggy in her yard. Chewie hopped up and rested his paws on the low windowsill and growled at the horse. "Now you jump into action," she joked, even though she wasn't in a jovial mood.

"This can't be good," she muttered. Becky paused at the mirror in her front hallway and glanced at herself. Dressed in sweats and a T-shirt with a messy bun, she had most definitely seen better days. She didn't want word swirling around the Amish community that she was falling apart. The bishop would probably use her as a cautionary tale. "Nothing good happens when you succumb to worldly pressures."

A familiar shame washed over her. *Be humble. Don't worry about what others think of you.*

A soft knock sounded again and Becky had to make a quick decision. Ignore the door or open it to see who was here.

Curiosity got the best of her.

She pulled open the door and sucked in a breath. "Mary Elizabeth." Paul's wife. The last time Becky had seen Mary was when they rescued Chewie from his horrible living conditions on the Kings' farm. Her old friend had been watching her from the porch when she left.

A thought suddenly slammed into her and she had an irrational urge to scoop up Chewie and hide him in the mudroom, but the fool dog was barking his head off at the horse. It wasn't like Becky could hide him now.

Mary bowed her bonneted head and clasped her hands together. Pink blossomed in her cheeks. Apparently, her old friend had found her house, but now that she was here, she couldn't find the words.

Becky stepped back and held out her hand. "Would you like to come in? I could make tea."

Mary studied her with cautious eyes. "I shouldn't." Her gaze scurried around the porch as if she feared she'd be discovered. "Can we talk out here?"

"Sure. Hold on." Becky closed the door over and ran to get Chewie's leash. She hooked it onto the ring of his collar and met Mary on the porch. She followed Chewie down the steps and stood on the walkway while Chewie sniffed and explored every inch of the yard that he possibly could within the parameters of his leash.

"I see the dog is doing well," Mary said, her voice soft.

"Yes. He seems happy." She studied her old friend. "What brings you here?"

Mary started wringing her hands again. "They came and took all the dogs away this morning."

Becky nodded, hiding her relief. "The dogs needed to be cared for. You must realize that."

"*Yah*, I do. And Paul does. He's too proud to admit we got overwhelmed. We never meant to let the conditions get so bad. After Paul's father died and we had a rough crop season, he thought it would be a way to make a little extra money." She turned her back to Becky, the hem of her long gown brushing against her black boots.

"Animal control will make sure they're cared for. It'll be fine."

"*Yah*, but I'm worried about my family. Will the sheriff's department take Paul away? He was only trying to do right by his family."

Becky tightened her grip as Chewie tugged, trying to chase a bunny under the tree but was foiled by the leash.

"Everything will be okay," Becky said reassuringly, but really, she had no idea what if any charges would be made.

"We heard *Englischers* liked puppies and were willing to pay *gut* money. We never…" She bowed her bonneted head. "We never meant to mistreat the dogs."

"What did the deputies say after they collected the animals?"

"I don't know. Paul told me to stay in the house." Mary's eyes grew wide. "I don't know how any of this works. I could never imagine the farm without him. We've already had a rough year." Every possible emotion flickered across her face as she considered the worst possible scenario.

"Don't borrow trouble."

"Can you talk to the sheriff? Make sure Paul isn't arrested? You can do that, *yah*?"

Becky dragged the toe of her sneaker along the edge of a paver. She wasn't sure how much she could do now that she was suspended, but her heart went out to her friend.

She took a chance. "I've been suspended from my job."

All the color seemed to drain from Mary's face. Her skin tone matched her bonnet. She turned away, then turned back around. "Was it because of the incident with Elijah Lapp?"

Becky studied her friend's face. *Does Mary know something?* A slow *whoosh-whoosh-whoosh* filled Becky's ears and she chose her next words carefully. "The sheriff is trying to sort out what happened. A video suggests I was more involved than I claimed." Her pulse spike with the injustice of it all. "But I'm innocent. I never hurt Elijah. I need a witness to come forward to support my claim." Her mouth grew dry, making it difficult to swallow.

"A witness?" Something about the way Mary said the two simple words niggled at Becky's insides. Anticipation buzzed her nerves.

Mary does know something.

"Can you help me?" Becky pressed her lips together, trying not to say too much. Trying not to scare her skittish friend.

Mary folded her arms tightly over the white bib of her pale gray dress and began to pace. "Maybe we can help each other." She flicked her gaze at Becky, then back down to the grass.

Becky waited.

"Paul's brother, Amos, was there the day Elijah got hurt. I'm sure he'd come forward as your witness if it meant protecting his brother."

A mix of hope and disbelief washed over Becky. "Does Amos know what happened?"

Mary drew up her shoulders and let them fall. "I heard Amos and Paul talking. Amos showed Paul the video."

"When did this happen?" Becky felt light-headed.

"Last week."

Becky's stomach bottomed out. "Are you sure?" Last week? Becky had only been suspended a few days ago.

"*Yah*, definitely. We had to clear out the barn for Sunday service and they were standing in the corner looking at something on Amos's phone."

"Do you know if Paul or Amos sent this video to anyone?" Deputy Reich's attorney had supposedly received it anonymously. Had Paul turned it over in an effort to get back at her for harassing—as he called it—him over the dogs? That had been an ongoing source of confrontation even before the Elijah incident. The video might have been the perfect ammunition Paul needed to get back at her.

Becky pressed a shaky hand to her forehead. If Paul thought the video would hurt her, how did Becky think Amos could help her now? A headache started behind her eyes, realizing the futility of it all. Unless… Unless, she thought to herself, Amos saw something the video hadn't captured. Maybe he could testify that she hadn't struck Elijah with her baton.

Nerves knotted her stomach. "Did Paul turn that video in to anyone? Maybe the lawyer representing the other deputy?"

"I don't know," she whispered.

"Why would Amos help me if he took the video? If he turned it in…" She scratched the top of her head. "He never came forward before. Why would he help now?"

"The men stopped talking when I approached, but I got the sense that Amos saw more than he videotaped." She studied the palm of her hand for a moment before continuing. "I know we lead very different lives now, but I know you'd never hurt someone."

"Thank you." New hope blossomed in Becky's chest and made her jittery. She had to act on this. "I need to talk to Amos. Get him to come forward." She watched Mary's face, praying that her friend might pave the way.

"Then you'll help Paul?"

"I'll see what I can do."

Mary's eyes brightened. "Really?"

"I can't promise you anything, but perhaps since the animals are now safe and healthy, he can pay a fine. Nothing more. I'll have to see. I don't have the power to make this decision."

"Denki." Mary nodded enthusiastically, perhaps overestimating Becky's influence.

"Don't tell Paul or Amos that you spoke with me, either," Becky said. She wanted to track down Amos this afternoon and use the element of surprise.

"Yah. I better go. I need to get dinner ready. Paul will be hungry." Without saying anything more, Mary turned and hustled toward her buggy, a woman on a mission. She unwound the reins from the light post near the end of the driveway. She hopped up on the buggy and flicked the reins. The horse began his steady trot.

Becky stared after the horse and buggy long after it disappeared, the *clip-clop-clip* ringing in her ears.

"Come on, Chewie. Time to go in." Her new companion bounded up the steps and sat down at the front door. Becky opened the door and the cool air-conditioning washed over her.

She unhooked the leash and patted Chewie on the head. He curled up on the couch. He lifted his head as if to beckon her. She plopped down next to him. The dog was great company, but she missed true companionship.

In just the past few days, she had talked to two Amish friends. Girls with whom she had shared a past. Her childhood hopes and dreams. She had missed their friendship. Was her past beckoning for her to return? Had she made a horrible mistake by leaving the only people who ever truly supported her?

She snapped off the TV and hugged her legs to her chest. She sat in silence save for the occasional jangle of Chewie's collar. She reached across and picked up her cell phone and texted Harrison.

Have lead on witness to Elijah's beating. Care to go with me?

She stretched to put the phone down when it chimed.

Yes, don't go alone. Pick you up after shift.

At the end of his shift, Harrison stopped by the sheriff's office. He was hoping for an update on the investigation into the Elijah Lapp beating as well as any news regarding the young men conducting target practice behind Becky's house.

Harrison lingered outside the office door, waiting for Sheriff Landry to finish up a phone call. He didn't want to appear to be eavesdropping.

Landry hung up the phone and looked up. "How can I help you?"

Harrison stepped inside the office and closed the door. "It's about Deputy Becky Spoth," he said, sitting down. He didn't want Landry to feel on the defensive.

Landry braced both hands on either side of his desk as he pushed back in the large leather chair without standing up. "I can't talk about the investigation. It's ongoing."

"I understand the difficult position you're in."

Landry sighed and slumped back in his chair as if he had finally found an ally. "This is the last thing I wanted during the first year of my tenure as sheriff."

His gaze drifted toward the door as if someone might overhear his confession.

Harrison cleared his throat. "Deputy Spoth needs support. I haven't known her for long, but I understand she grew up Amish." Harrison was reluctant to reveal his growing relationship with Becky for no other reason than to respect her privacy.

"Yes?" The curious inflection in the single word suggested the sheriff wanted to know what one had to do with the other.

"Becky walked away from her community and she no longer has their support." Harrison drummed his fingers on his thigh, feeling a current of anxiety. "Now she doesn't feel like she has the support of the department." In a sense, she was being shamed from all sides. Harrison imagined that was how his brother felt during his downward spiral before his death.

Landry sighed heavily. "She's in a tough spot. She testified against another officer and then a video surfaced suggesting she may have been just as guilty."

"Is that what you believe?" Harrison struggled to keep his voice even. "That she's guilty?"

Landry steepled his fingers and placed his elbows on the desk, and gave him a bland, non-committal expression as if debating which path would have the least negative effect on his career. Protecting one's own backside seemed to be a natural political instinct.

"The video is damaging to her story," the sheriff said evenly.

"We can't…" Harrison braced his hands on the arms of the chair to stand, then decided to lean back. *Deep breath. Control your anger.* "Any chance there are other witnesses? Someone who saw more than the video showed?" He wanted to get the inside dirt before meeting with Becky and discussing her possible witness.

Landry ran a hand over his mouth. "The deputies have canvassed the community. Nothing. The Amish are tight-lipped. I don't imagine it's going to be easy, especially since Becky used to be one of them. They already view her as a traitor."

"What would it take to get her back in uniform, because we both know she's innocent in this."

A corner of the sheriff's mouth twitched. "She's going to have to be patient as we investigate."

"Do you really think—" he stopped short of calling her Becky "—Deputy Spoth is a bad deputy?" A growing anger pulsed in his veins at the sheriff's cool indifference, or so it seemed.

Landry lifted his palms. "I don't. But it's hard to dispute a damaging video."

Harrison cleared his throat. "The video shows nothing." He had seen a copy floating around the department.

"It's inconclusive. We can't have it blow back in our faces if she's found guilty. We can't appear too soft because she's a woman. Or former Amish. This needs to be done by the book."

"Investigate, then. Do what you need to, but in the meantime, also be aware that someone is trying to hurt Becky."

"Hurt?" The sheriff jerked his head back. "She reported that someone slashed her tires in the lot here. It's certainly not a common occurrence, but it's not rare, either. We live in a small town. Teenagers get bored." He leaned forward, resting his forearms on the desk. "They do stupid stuff."

"You can't blame this on kids will be kids."

Landry's brows snapped together. "And the Buffalo incident can't be related to this."

They didn't know that for sure. "What about the incident in her yard when she almost got shot?" He struggled to keep his frustration in check.

"Some young men were having target practice. They neglected to show you all their guns." The sheriff seemed to be able to explain everything away.

"Did anyone follow up with them?" Harrison couldn't find anything in the system, but the deputy in charge of the investigation could have looked deeper into their stories.

The sheriff flattened his hands on the desk. "Nope. Nothing. I'm thinking that's a dead end."

Harrison stared at him a long minute, deciding how to proceed on that. Is this what small-town policing was like?

"Listen," the sheriff said, having gone back to tapping the pads of his fingers together, "I know you want to help, but we have to be careful. We have to root out bad deputies, otherwise it makes the whole department look bad. Quail Hollow is still reeling from one of its own murdering a young Amish mother."

"That happened decades ago." Harrison had only recently moved to Quail Hollow when news broke of the arrest of a former undersheriff in the murder of a young Amish mother over two decades ago. Allegations that the sheriff's department didn't know how to police their own were splashed all over the news from Buffalo to Cleveland. Now it seemed Becky would pay the price for stricter policing among their own.

"The truth was hidden for a long time. As the new

sheriff, my campaign promise was to be transparent. I can't shirk my duty because it's tough. People have long memories."

Harrison had the same convictions when it came to his brother. Tough love and all that. Sometimes living with the effects of your convictions was harder than having the convictions in the first place.

"We'll follow up on everything, Deputy James," the sheriff said, a dismissal clear in his tone. "Best if you stay out of it. It seems you might be biased."

Heat flared in his ears, but he bit back his temper. "Deputy Spoth needs to be cleared sooner rather than later."

Landry held up his arms with his wrists together, miming that his hands were tied. Harrison took it as an excuse to do nothing.

Harrison pushed to his feet. "Sometimes *someone* has to stand up for what's right, even if their hands are tied."

Landry got to his feet. The cords straining in his neck suggested he, too, was holding back the full force of his temper. "Are you suggesting I'm not doing my job?" He tapped his index finger on the desk repeatedly for emphasis. "I'm the sheriff here. My job is to find the truth. Not fly off the handle because I don't think one of my female deputies is capable of excessive force." He lowered his voice to a low growl. "They want equal rights, now they have them and can't handle the consequences."

It was Harrison's turn to narrow his gaze. "I'd almost think you had something against women in the department."

The sheriff's eyes widened, looking like he had been

offended. "I don't care if my deputies are male or female. I only care that they do their jobs." He paused for effect. "This department can't afford another black eye."

Harrison turned toward the door, then turned back. "In your efforts to protect this department, don't forget to focus on protecting the people that work within it."

The sheriff leaned back and crossed his arms, the expression revealing his barely contained rage.

As soon as Harrison pulled up the driveway, Becky ran across the lawn and hopped into his truck. She was glad to see he had changed into jeans and a T-shirt, because it would make approaching Amos King easier. He might talk if he felt less threatened.

She still couldn't believe she had a potential witness.

"Thanks for coming," she said. "I would have followed up on this myself, but your lawyer friend said I shouldn't do anything to stir the pot regarding my case, and this definitely feels like stirring the pot." She resisted reaching out and tapping his arm, she was so excited.

Harrison put the truck into Reverse. "Where to?"

"Let's try the church parking lot on Main Street. I've seen Amos with his friends riding skateboards down there. It's worth a shot. This way we don't have to confront him at home in front of his brother, Paul."

Harrison pulled out onto the road and headed into town. "So Amos is part of the King family?"

"Yes. Amos is Paul's younger brother."

"Interesting. There are only a few degrees of separation around here."

"You don't know the half of it."

"Tell me what happened. This Amos kid took the

video, but his brother Paul turned it in anonymously to give you grief because you've been on him about the dogs? Did I get that right?" Becky had shared the events of this afternoon over the phone.

"Mary didn't say Paul turned it in, but it had to be him. Amos doesn't have any ill feelings toward me. There's no reason." She searched her memory, but couldn't come up with anything.

When they got to the church, sure enough, a handful of young men were using the stairs, railings and parking curbs to do stunts.

"Pull over here. I don't want them to take off if they see us coming," Becky said.

"Do you see Amos?" Harrison asked.

Squinting, Becky leaned forward. The early-evening sun was right in her line of vision. A tall guy leaped off the stairs and landed on his skateboard, rolled a few feet before spinning around to watch a friend repeat the stunt behind him. His blunt-cut hair poked out from under a Buffalo Bills baseball cap. The frayed edges spoke of its age.

"The kid on the right. I think that's him. Come on." She pushed open the door without waiting for him.

When Becky was within a few feet, she called Amos's name. He stepped on the back of the skateboard and it popped up into his hand. "Yeah," he started to say, rather coolly, until recognition sparked in his eyes. "Hey, Rebecca." If she wasn't watching him so closely, she might have missed the color growing in his cheeks.

She pointed at his skateboard. "You're pretty good at that." Amos was a handful of years younger than Paul. He had always looked up to his brother while Paul seemed to dismiss him. She supposed that dynamic was fairly universal, Amish or not, big brother to little brother.

"I want to talk to you about a video."

Amos tucked the skateboard under his arm and dipped his head. His bangs hid his eyes. "I don't know what you're talking about," he mumbled with the lilt of Pennsylvania Dutch.

"I think you do." Becky took another step toward him, then she suddenly changed tactics. "I'm hoping you can help me." She also hoped all the times she had been nice to Paul's younger brother would pay off here.

The other three boys stopped doing stunts in the church lot long enough to watch them. "We're just chatting," Becky said in her best reassuring tone. "You guys can go about your business. All I want to do is talk to Amos."

One of the kids' eyes suddenly lit up and he pointed frantically at her. Was that admiration she detected in his eyes? "You're the lady deputy who beat up Elijah."

"Are you basing that on something you witnessed firsthand?" Harrison asked, speaking up before Becky had a chance to find her voice. Regardless of her innocence, would she forever be known as the "lady deputy who beat up the Amish kid"? She tried to hide her frustration by squaring her shoulders and never taking her eyes off Amos's friend.

"No, um…" The kid started to stammer. "I saw the video. It went viral. Totally awesome." If violent videos were deemed awesome, Becky feared for the next generation. She clenched her teeth, fighting the urge to school the young men. There was nothing awesome about it. But she couldn't risk Amos shutting down.

"Did you post the video online?" Becky asked.

"No, but I recorded it." Amos pushed the gravel around with the toe of his sneaker. He probably had a stash of clothes and shoes at a friend's house that he changed in and out of as he left home, not wanting to get any grief from Paul or Mary. Amos was the last unmarried King. From what Becky's sister had told her, Amos was supposed to be baptized and married later this year. He certainly didn't act like a young man preparing for baptism and subsequent marriage in an Amish community. "And I sent it to a bunch of people, too." He looked up with a hint of regret in his eyes. "It was just a video."

Just a video that had ruined her life.

She drew in a deep breath to calm her rioting nerves. "Okay, so someone alerted Deputy Reich's lawyer about the video. That can't be undone. But I could use your help, Amos." She took a step closer, forcing him to meet her gaze, reminding him who she was. "Did you see the entire incident with Elijah?"

"Yah." He looked up, a wary look in his eyes.

Her mouth went dry. Had she found her witness? *Please, Lord.* She held her breath and dared to ask him the question. "Did you see me hurt Elijah Lapp?"

Amos shook his head slowly. *"Neh."*

"What did you see?"

Amos rubbed his nose vigorously. "You used a stick to pry the deputy off Elijah. When you pulled him off, he landed on you, but you scrabbled out from under him and forced him back down."

"You saw all this?"

"Yah, when I was running away. The video caught the ground, but I didn't take my eyes off the fight. By

the time I got to the Millers' barn, the other patrol cars and the ambulance had arrived."

Thank you, Lord.

"What were you doing at the Millers' farm?"

"They hired me to do some extra work."

Becky considered all this. "Would you be willing to come down to the sheriff's department and give your testimony?"

"Oh, man. I don't know. I'm supposed to be preparing for baptism. How am I going to explain having a cell phone and taking videos? The bishop won't think I'm serious about committing to the Amish."

"I'll do all I can to protect you. I need your help."

Amos looked like he was going to be sick.

"Please, Amos. The truth needs to be told. Someone is trying to hurt me and I'm afraid it's because they think I hurt Elijah."

Amos opened his mouth to protest, but Becky's smile seemed to disarm him.

"Someone slashed my tires. Someone shot at my house."

"I don't know anything about that. I just took the video. That's all. I promise."

"Of course," Becky said. "And I'm sure you had nothing to do with the dogs in your family's barn."

Amos's eyes lit up. "No way. That was all Paul. I told him it was a bad idea. I'd leave the cage open at times, letting them get away."

That explained how Chewie got out.

"Besides," Amos added, seeming skittish, "the deputies took the dogs away."

"I know," Becky said.

"But why did you show Paul the video?" Harrison asked.

Amos's gaze skittered over to him. "I showed it to a lot of people. And it was on the internet."

"Have you heard any rumors about me?" Becky calmly drew his attention back to her. "Perhaps someone wanted to get back at me for hurting Elijah?"

Fear flickered in Amos's watchful brown eyes. *"Neh."*

Harrison tapped the screen of his cell phone and brought up the photos of the four men shooting targets behind her house. "Do you know these guys?"

Amos stared at the screen. *"Yah,* I've seen them all around town."

"Where exactly?" Harrison pressed.

Amos explained how he knew each of the guys and added a bit on whether he liked them or not. Becky and Harrison both let him keep talking, figuring he might unwittingly reveal something important.

At one of the photos, Amos said, "That kid is the sheriff's nephew."

Harrison jerked his head back. "Interesting. What kind of kid is he?"

Amos hitched a shoulder. "Tyler seems all right. Us guys don't really discuss much."

"Is he a troublemaker?" Harrison asked.

"Depends on what you call trouble." Amos smirked. "From where I come from, riding a skateboard and doing stunts could be construed as trouble."

"Has Tyler been in any kind of trouble?" Becky clarified.

"All I know is that he grew up in Buffalo and his mother sent him to live with his uncle, the sheriff, to straighten him out." Amos pulled off his hat, adjusted the bill and stuffed it back down on his head. "I imagine that means he got into some kind of trouble back home. That's all I know."

"Thanks." Becky shot Harrison a quick gaze. Not wanting to scare Amos off, she handed him a business card. "I could really use your help. Call me if you're willing to come in as a witness."

"Ah, man," he groaned again, but she could tell he was softening. He'd come through for her; she just knew it.

"If you don't want to deal with me, go directly to the sheriff's department and ask for the sheriff." Becky touched Harrison's elbow. "Let's go."

When they reached the car, Becky said, "I think he'll come around."

Harrison nodded. "I hope so. But why didn't the sheriff tell me Tyler was his nephew when I showed him his photo?"

A knot tightened in Becky's gut. "Does this mean we can't trust the sheriff?"

"It means someone's holding out on us. It means we have to investigate ourselves. We can't leave it to the sheriff's department."

TEN

"We're going to have to look into the sheriff's nephew," Becky said as Harrison drove her home.

"I ran all four guys' names through the system. Nothing came up."

"Mind if I look at the photos again?" Becky asked.

Without taking his eyes off the road, Harrison took his phone out of the cup holder and handed it to her. He pressed his thumb on the button to unlock it. "Go to the photo app."

"Mind if I send the images to my phone?"

"Go ahead. Just not quite sure what we're going to uncover since none of them have records. Someone needs to start talking."

"Amos is a start." She pressed her lips together. "Should we go to each of these guys' homes? Talk to them directly?"

Harrison scrubbed his hand across his face. "Let me see what I can dig up on the sheriff's nephew first. If we start asking too many of the guys questions, they might start talking to each other and shut down. Then we'll get nowhere."

Becky sighed heavily. "I feel like we're already getting nowhere. I'm—"

Her phone rang in her hand as she was saving the photos she had sent to her phone, stopping her midsentence. "It's my sister. I better get this."

Becky lifted the phone to her ear. "Hi, Mag."

"Bec-ky." her sister said her name on a sob.

Becky's heart dropped to her shoes. "What's wrong?"

"Paul said they're going to kill all the dogs they took from his farm and *Dat* told me it was none of my business and—"

"Stay where you are. I'll be right there."

"But *Dat* is mad. He'll be mad I called you."

Anger pulsed through her veins. "I'm sorry, but this has gone on long enough. I'll be right there." The thought of her sister alone in the barn, crying her eyes out while talking on their only landline, broke Becky's heart. She remembered feeling so alone and adrift while growing up on the Amish farm with no one to talk to. She didn't dare share her deepest thoughts about leaving.

Becky ended the call before Mag could argue. She looked over at Harrison, who cut her a gaze, then turned his attention back to the road. "Mind making a pit stop?"

"Whatever you want."

It took less than ten minutes to get to her family's farm. "Want me to park on the road, so my truck's not visible?"

"No, pull right into the driveway." Defiance laced her tone. "I don't care who sees us. They have no right…"

Becky jumped out of the truck before she finished her sentence. She jogged over to the barn and found Mag sitting on a hay bale in the shadows. The fading light of the setting sun created long lines across the barn floor.

Becky sat down next to her sister and put her arm around her shoulders. At this moment Mag seemed so much younger than her seventeen years. She stiffened for a fraction before accepting the gesture and resting her bonneted head on her sister's shoulder.

"Tell me what happened?"

"The deputies took the puppies this morning."

"Paul wasn't taking care of them. You know that." She nudged her sister's shoulder affectionately. "And now I'm blessed to have Chewie."

"That's a silly name for a dog," Mag said distractedly.

"But appropriate." Becky lifted an eyebrow.

Mag shook her head, and her lips started to quiver again. "Paul told me that the deputies put the dogs into bags with rocks and drown them."

Shock pulsed through Becky's veins. She didn't think she could be any more angry with anyone ever than she was with Paul right now.

"That's not true. No one's going to hurt those dogs. They'll make sure they're cared for and then they'll search for homes for them."

"He said you'd lie about it. He said they had to drown them because they don't have resources to care for so many puppies." She drew in a shaky breath. "He said he was getting around to cleaning up the cages. That he would have made things right. That it was my fault the puppies would get drowned."

Mag's grief-stricken words bounced around Becky's brain. "I can't believe—" She couldn't think straight. She wanted to run over to the Kings' farm and give Paul a piece of her mind. How dare he strike terror into Mag's heart with his lies? Was he that angry at her that he'd take it out on her sister?

Mag sat up and swiped at her cheeks. "You have to get the dogs back. I'll never forgive myself if they kill them."

"They're not going to kill them." A horrible realization swept over Becky. Her sister believed Paul over her own flesh and blood. Mag believed an Amish man instead of her own sister, an outsider.

The reality of the moment settled on Becky's lungs and made it difficult to breathe.

She took a moment to compose herself, fearing if she spoke, her sister would hear the hurt in her voice. Her sister didn't need any more guilt heaped on her already aching heart.

"Let's talk to my friend Harrison. He knows the man who picked up the Kings' dogs. He can assure you that they'll care for the animals until they find new homes." Becky stood and held out her hand to pull her sister to her feet.

"How do I know he's not lying?" Mag stood without taking her hand.

"You're going to have to trust me."

In front of Becky's childhood home, Harrison waited by the truck. After a short time, he saw two shadows emerge from the barn. As they got closer, he noticed Becky had her arm around her crying sister.

"Everything okay?" he asked.

"No, it's not." Becky's words came out clipped and he could tell she was angry. Maybe even a little hurt. "Can you call Deputy Timothy Welsh? I need him to assure Mag that the dogs confiscated from the King property will be better cared for than when they were caged up next door."

"Yes, sure." Harrison's gaze drifted to Mag and then back to Becky. As he was entering "Welsh" in his contacts on his smartphone, a crash made all three of them jump.

A tall, thin man with a long beard emerged from the house, the force of his exit slamming the screen door against the side of the house. He didn't slow down for the woman scurrying behind him as he strode across the hard-packed earth toward them. A dent ringed his hair and forehead where his hat once sat. Harrison could easily assume this was Becky's father.

"What's going on here?" he demanded, his voice gruff, his jaw set for battle.

Mag refused to meet her father's gaze. Her chin trembled. "I-I called Becky to see if she could get the Kings' dogs back. I don't want for them to be drowned."

"Your sister has done enough." Mr. Spoth pointed at Becky, then the truck. "Get out of here."

The hurt in Becky's eyes cut through Harrison. He understood what it was like to have a family ripped apart.

"Dat," Becky said, twisting her hands in front of her, then letting them drop and squaring her shoulders. She returned her father's unwavering gaze. "We're going to make a phone call to assure Mag that the animals are okay. Then I'll go."

Mr. Spoth's nostrils flared. "You had no right to

interfere in Paul's business. You chose to leave. Your life isn't with us. Now go."

"Sir," Harrison said, daring to step forward. "Your daughter and I were worried about the well-being of the dogs. We had a responsibility to make sure they weren't being mistreated."

Mr. Spoth laughed harshly. "Responsibilities. My daughter knows nothing about responsibilities. We raised her to choose baptism and marriage within the Amish community. Then she shamed us by leaving in the middle of the night. She doesn't care what goes on around here. You have been corrupted by outside influences." Mr. Spoth blinked slowly. "We can't have her infecting our other daughter with her dangerous attitudes. She shamed us. We don't want anything to do with her unless she comes back to openly confess with a contrite heart."

Becky audibly gasped as if she had been sucker punched, but she didn't speak up to defend herself. Harrison assumed long-established father-daughter boundaries were at play here, not allowing her to find her words. To speak up against her father.

Familiar feelings crowded in on Harrison's heart, making him share Becky's shock, but not at her father's outburst, but at his own actions, not unlike the harshness of her father. Harrison understood the feelings of hurt and shame that allowed a person to alienate someone they loved. He lived those emotions with his brother.

Harrison couldn't stay silent.

"I'm not Amish, sir, but I can assure you I understand family and how important it is."

Mr. Spoth turned his head, his strong profile outlined against the purples and oranges of the evening sky. His posture suggested he wanted nothing to do with Harrison, but he hadn't walked away, either. Harrison's gaze drifted to the porch where Mrs. Spoth stood very still, as if afraid to move.

"I know what it's like to be disappointed by a family member. I know what it's like to push them out of my life. To try to get them to see the error of their ways." Harrison coughed to clear the emotion from his throat. "Unfortunately, I know what it's like to lose that person forever. And I'm not talking because he moved across town. My brother is dead and I did nothing to help him before he reached that point."

He felt Becky's warm hand on his forearm, but he couldn't meet her eyes. His heart was racing in his ears.

"I am sorry for your brother, but you are not Amish. You could never understand," Mr. Spoth bit out.

"Perhaps," Harrison conceded. "But you have your daughter right here. She's made a decision you don't care for, but she's trying to help the daughter that is here. I suggest you accept the offer in whatever way doesn't offend the rules you live by. But I imagine your God is the same God my mother taught me to pray to, and He'd want you to accept your daughter for who she is."

"Perhaps you forgot your lessons, son. The fourth commandment says honor your father and mother. Our daughter shamed us."

Becky squeezed Harrison's arm. "Let's go." She turned toward her sister. "I promise you the dogs are okay. I'll call the deputy who picked them up and check on them." She walked around to the passenger side of the vehicle. "Trust me."

"Good night," Harrison said curtly, and climbed into the truck and slammed the door.

Becky slumped into the passenger seat of his truck and snapped on her seat belt. Her heart was racing so hard she thought it was going to jump out of her chest. She had never had a confrontation with her father. Not like that. Since she left, their relationship was non-existent or if their paths accidentally crossed in town, he pretended he didn't see her.

Sadness and anger threaded around her middle and made it difficult to breathe. She focused straight ahead, ignoring the hard stare of her father as Harrison did a wide U-turn in the driveway and pulled out onto the main road. She tried not to notice her mother in the shadows of the porch, slump-shouldered and silent. Always silent.

"I probably should have kept my mouth shut. I'm sure I didn't help any," Harrison said, his voice low and somber.

She shifted in her seat to face him, the shadow of a beard on his jaw. The urge to reach over and cup his chin and reassure him was strong, but she wasn't that kind of person. She was a person who had grown up Amish, with conservative values, who was now struggling to fit into her new world. Yet feeling like she was doing a miserable job at that, too.

"Thank you for sticking up for me."

"I didn't mean to be disrespectful. It's just…" He stared straight ahead, letting his words trail off. "It bothers me that he won't acknowledge you when you're right there."

"It's their way. We've talked about it. They hope I'll

come back." She curled her fingers around the edge of the seat. "Are you really that angry with God?" It made her heart sad to hear the words he had chosen when confronting her *dat*.

Harrison's Adam's apple bobbed as he seemed to consider her question.

"I didn't mean to pry. You don't have to answer."

"I suppose I can't get past why God would let my brother die in such a horrible..." He shook his head.

She threaded her fingers together. "I'm sorry you're hurting. Everyone has free will. To make choices. Your brother made some horrible decisions. You can't punish yourself for the rest of your life because of *his* choices."

"I thought I was doing the right thing by showing my brother how mad I was." He stared straight ahead at the road, but he seemed lost in thought.

She reached across and touched his arm. "You can't undo what's already happened. If your brother was anything like you, I don't think he'd want you to punish yourself for the rest of your life."

"No." The single word wasn't convincing. "Do you ever regret leaving?"

Harrison's question surprised her as much as the answer that sprang to her lips. "Lately I've wondered. The Amish are all about community. I felt the sheriff's department was also a supportive community until I really needed that support. Then everyone disappeared. Even my friend, Anne, the sheriff's administrative assistant, has stopped returning my calls. Everyone I thought was a friend has disappeared." She laughed, a mirthless sound. "But then again, others have shown friendship when they didn't have to." She squeezed his arm. "Thank you for that."

"Of course." Harrison cut her a quick gaze before returning his attention to the dark country road. "Would you ever consider going back?"

"To the Amish? No, I couldn't be happy living in the Amish way. I know that for certain. Despite everything." *I've come too far. Yet, not far enough.*

The reality of that pained her heart. She was like an orphan without a home. "I guess that means I have to work extra hard to clear my name."

ELEVEN

The next day Becky was determined not to sit around feeling sorry for herself. Chewie was a big help with that. "Come on, let's go outside. Get some air."

She hooked his leash on his collar and he charged ahead toward the back door. He bounded down the steps and over to the tree line. A hint of unease whispered across the back of her neck. Would she ever feel safe again? Or would she forever be looking over her shoulder?

She said a silent prayer that the sheriff's department would find the person who was harassing her. Maybe then she wouldn't feel so jittery.

"Maybe it's time to weed the flower beds," Becky said to Chewie. "Get this place looking nice." That was one thing she loved about being independent. She had her own house that she could maintain. And she could do the chores when and if she felt like it.

She bent down and wrapped the end of the dog's leash around one of the posts on the railing. She tugged on it to make sure it was secure. She opened the small shed and found her gardening gloves. She tapped them together and little balls of dirt sprinkled to the ground.

She studied the shelves until she located the long tool with a pronged end used for weed removal. "What else do I need?" She tucked a paper compost bag under her elbow, then closed over the shed door.

Standing directly on the other side was Deputy Ned Reich. Based on his expression, she wasn't sure who was more surprised.

"Ned," she said, her voice cracking. The man she had testified against. The man who had beaten an Amish man to within an inch of his life.

"I didn't mean to startle you," he said, his expression now stoic.

Her heart thrummed in her ears and she swallowed around a too-tight throat. Could she beat him to the back door? She cut a sideways glance to Chewie, who seemed more interested in sniffing around the base of a tree than her predicament.

Ned lifted his hand toward the house. "I rang the doorbell and knocked, but no one answered. I saw your car in the driveway, so I thought I'd walk around." He stuffed his hands in his pockets and rolled back on his heels.

Despite his nonthreatening manner, her instincts were to grip the long, metal tool tighter. He seemed to sense that and his gaze dropped to her white-knuckled fist.

"I assure you, you don't need that," he said in a deep, even tone, but something in his eyes gave her pause.

Becky eased her posture, trying not to show fear. Her thoughts raced and she swallowed hard. She stared back at him with what she hoped was a neutral stare. "How can I help you?"

"I suppose I could say you've helped enough." He

ran a hand over his face. "But that's not why I'm here. I wanted to let you know that I've talked to Sheriff Landry."

"I didn't think anything was going on right now with your case."

"It's not about that. Well, it is, but not anything official right now. I needed to take responsibility for what I did."

Becky blinked rapidly, trying to make sense of what he was saying.

"I know I'm a hothead. I've always been a hothead. But I need to take responsibility. I can't let you continue to pay for what I did."

"Really?" she whispered, not sure if she had given voice to the single word.

"Your only crime was rolling up on the scene as my backup. You weren't involved in the beating—" he tilted his head "—except for breaking it up." A hint of amusement flashed in his eyes as if he had sensed the irony of his words.

Becky pressed her hand to her chest and the tip of the weeding tool tapped her chin. "Why? Why come forward now?"

Ned scratched his eyebrow and studied the ground for a moment before lifting his gaze and meeting hers. "I've destroyed my career and I'm feeling pretty down and out." He cleared his throat as if he was touching on stuff that he didn't usually discuss. "And my lawyer encouraged me to see a counselor regarding anger management." He hitched a shoulder. "Thought it would look good when it came to the trial—that I was seeking counseling and truly sorry."

"Are you?"

A muscle twitched in his jaw. "I'm sorry I let it get to this, yeah." He twisted his lips into a wry grin and ran his palm over the back of his neck. "In talking to the counselor, I realized it wasn't fair to you. You seem like a good person. I'm going down, but I can't take you with me."

"Thank you." Becky set her gardening tool on the shelf in the cabinet, then peeled off her gloves.

"I just came from the sheriff's office and thought you'd like to know. I expect my lawyer won't be happy about it." He cleared his throat. "But I truly believe now, looking back, that you've saved me from facing more serious charges." He shook his head as if reliving the event that had changed the course of both their lives. "I was so angry. I saw how close Lapp had come to hitting that kid crossing the road... I would have killed Elijah Lapp if you hadn't intervened."

"Thank you for letting me know," she said. "What did the sheriff say?" *Does this mean I'm getting my job back?*

"He took my statement. Didn't fill me in on his next steps. I suppose I won't ever be privy to his plans." He shrugged again and took a step backward as if ready to retreat.

"Do you want to come in for an iced tea?"

Before he had a chance to answer, her cell phone in her back pocket rang. Her first instinct was to ignore it, but something told her to answer it. "Can you hold on one second?" She pulled it out and glanced at the display and then Ned. "It's a call coming from the sheriff's department."

"Take it," Ned said. "Maybe it's good news."

"Hello." Becky listened intently while the sheriff

confirmed what Ned had told her. For some reason she didn't feel the need to tell the sheriff that Ned was standing right in front of her.

Just when she thought the sheriff was finishing up, he said, "Amos King came in today, too."

"He did?" Becky took a step back into the shade. The top of her hair had grown hot from the sun.

"Told me he witnessed the whole thing. Confirmed much of what Ned had said."

Becky didn't know what to say.

"I'm not sure who this lawyer you hired is, but he's pulled a few rabbits out of the hat for you."

Something about his comment made her bristle. The sheriff hadn't exactly been forthcoming when it came to investigating the incidents following her suspension. From the start, his focus seemed to be on keeping his own reputation intact. She struggled to keep her tone even. "My lawyer had nothing to do with the two individuals who came forward."

The sheriff didn't say anything, so she continued, "Any news on my slashed tires or the shooting behind my house?" She felt Ned's gaze on her, even with her back to him.

"Working on it." Becky imagined him tapping the pads of his fingers together like he always seemed to do when he was giving her a speech in his office. "Maybe a witness will wander in and solve the case for me." Becky didn't miss the hint of derision in his tone.

Ned started to walk away and she held up her finger, indicating that he hold on a minute. Then into the phone, "When can I return to work?"

"I need a few days to fill out paperwork. I'm thinking Monday."

"Monday would be great. See you then." Becky ended the call, not giving him a chance to prolong her return to work any longer.

"Your suspension has been lifted?" Ned asked, a hint of relief in his voice.

"Yes. I go back Monday. Apparently, another witness came in today and confirmed that I only used the baton to pry you and Elijah apart."

Ned plowed his hand through his unkempt hair. Now that Becky thought about it, he looked like he had just rolled out of bed. Or off the couch. A little part of her could relate. The world could get awfully small when you lost your job under these circumstances. She wondered where Ned would go from here.

"I'm glad to hear it." He sounded sincere. "I'll let you have at it." He gestured with his chin toward the shed and her gardening tools.

Before he had a chance to walk away, she asked, "What now?"

"Ask for mercy. Probably have to find a new job."

Becky opened her mouth to say sorry, then clamped it shut again. Apologizing couldn't be her default answer. She had nothing to be sorry about. "Do you have a good support system at home?"

Ned laughed and his overall demeanor changed. "Now you're sounding like my shrink."

"I know what it's like to be left out in the cold."

"Well, my home life is a little messed up. I've never been much good on that front either. I'm afraid marriage number two is on the rocks." He took a deep breath. "And I'm sure you know my oldest son. He's a deputy."

Becky nodded, but didn't say anything.

"He's turning into a hothead like me. You'd think I'd serve as a cautionary tale. He better learn to check his emotions before he ruins his career and any relationship he might have."

Despite the mess this man had created for her, she felt compassion for him. Forgiveness. "Come in out of the heat. I have iced tea."

Ned held up his hand. "No, thanks. I really should go." He averted his gaze briefly, then looked at her, a sadness in his eyes. "I hope things work out for you."

"I hope things work out for you, too."

Apparently, the Amish tenet of forgiveness hadn't been something she had left behind when she jumped the fence.

"Are you ready to go back to work tomorrow?" Harrison lifted the glass of icy-cold lemonade to his lips and glanced over at Becky, her one leg folded under her in the rocking chair on her front porch. Chewie rested at her feet. In the front yard, a cloud of insects swirled over the grass, back lit by the purples and oranges of another gorgeous sunset.

The past few days since her name was cleared, he and Becky hadn't talked much. He figured he didn't have an excuse to visit. But now, with a return to work looming, he had taken the opportunity to stop by. To see how she was feeling.

Becky ran her hand up and down the arm of the chair. "I'm nervous. Feels almost like the first day."

"You shouldn't be nervous. You're a good deputy." He set the glass down on the table between them. "You stepped in and protected a young Amish man. You did what was right."

Becky used her toe to rock back and forth. She looked over at Chewie, careful not to crunch his tail under the rockers. "People will always associate me with the beating. People tend to only remember what they want to remember."

"You can't control what other people think."

She lifted an eyebrow as if to say, "Whatever." She traced a line of grain in the wood on the arm of the chair with her index finger. "I wonder if they'll ever find out who was harassing me. The sheriff claimed it would probably settle down now that a witness had come forward. He thinks it was someone trying to get back at me for hurting Elijah, but now that I've been cleared, they have no reason to come after me." She tilted her head and ran her fingers through her long ponytail. "But the sheriff assures me they're still investigating."

"They won't let someone get away with it."

"No, I suppose not. I wish everything could be wrapped up so these reporters stop calling me. They're like vultures."

"Crimes among the Amish are big news."

"Unfortunately."

"It'll die down." Harrison reassured her.

Becky stifled a yawn and Harrison stood. "I should get going."

"Sorry." She bowed her head. "I didn't mean to be rude by yawning."

"I hope we can still be friends."

Becky crossed her arms, but didn't meet his gaze. She slowed her rocking. "Of course we can be friends." She stressed the word *friends* a bit too heavily. She wasn't interested in dating, so it didn't come as a surprise. "I appreciate all you've done for me." Pink blossomed in her cheeks.

"I didn't mean to make you uncomfortable…" Harrison was never this tongue-tied. "I hadn't made an effort to get to know people before now and I'm glad I took the time with you." They locked gazes. "It'll be nice to have a friendly face while I'm in Quail Hollow."

"You plan on leaving soon?" Some emotion he couldn't pinpoint flickered across her features.

"No, not soon, but I can't avoid the demons of my past forever. I'll have to go back to Buffalo. Clean out the house." He took a deep breath. "Maybe even beg for my old job back." He shrugged. "Find a new one, maybe? But I'm not in a hurry. I'd like to make sure whoever's harassing you is punished."

"I'd feel much better knowing they had someone in custody." She stood and tugged at the hem of her T-shirt.

Harrison brushed the back of his hand across the smooth skin of her arm. "Remember you're not alone." He bent and planted a kiss on her forehead. Then he stepped back and the space between them was charged with electricity.

Something caught Chewie's attention and he bolted from the porch. Becky darted in an attempt to catch the leash when a shot rang out. Instinctively, Harrison moved to protect Becky, pushing her down and toward the house for cover. A piercing pain radiated up his arm.

"In the house," he yelled at her. "Get in the house."

Her eyes grew wide with fear. As he shoved her toward the door, she pushed back, craning to see around him. "Chewie!"

Despite her resistance, Harrison opened the door and shoved her inside and slammed the door. "Stay away from the windows."

"Chewie's going to get lost." Frantic, she reached for the door handle.

"No." He lifted his hand to stop her. "We need to make sure it's clear." That was when he noticed blood running down his arm.

"Oh no…" All the color drained from Becky's face and suddenly he felt nauseated himself. "You've been hit. Sit." She pushed him against the wall and guided him to a seated position. "Stay put." She raced to the kitchen and returned with her cell phone and a dish towel.

She handed him the towel. "Hold this against the wound." Then she ran to the front of the house and peeked out the window. She glanced down at her phone and dialed. "This is Deputy Spoth. Shots have been fired at my residence." She rattled off the address. "Deputy James has been hit. Send an ambulance. Be cautious. Active shooter."

She ended the call, then ran back to Harrison. She took the dish towel from him and pressed it to his arm. "They could be hiding anywhere. There are too many trees around." As she crouched in front of him, he found himself studying her bright, blue eyes filled with concern. "Are you okay?"

"I think I'm okay." A buzzing started in his ears and he immediately realized that he had spoken too soon.

Becky pulled the towel back from his arm and twisted her mouth.

"Not much for blood?" he asked, trying to make light of the situation.

"Um, no…" She grimaced. "You'll need to go to the emergency room for sure. This isn't a do-it-yourself wound. The ambulance should be here soon."

The glass on the front window exploded. Instinctively, Harrison pushed to his feet and moved them both toward the center of the house. "Stay away from any windows." He glanced around, anticipating his next move if the shooter tried to gain entry. "Where's the gun I left you?"

Hunched over, Becky scrambled upstairs to retrieve the gun from the safe in her bedroom, careful to stay clear of the windows. The sheriff had returned her gun and badge on Friday in preparation for Monday. Holding the weapon at the ready, she positioned herself next to the broken window on the first level of the house. Making sure she didn't create a target, she peeked out of a corner of the window, her gaze scanning the heavily shadowed yard. The gunman could be anywhere.

And Chewie was nowhere in sight. She prayed he was hunkered down behind a tree. But the silence unnerved her. She expected him to be barking, at the very least.

"You okay?" she hollered to Harrison, who was sitting against the wall in the dining room.

"I've been better," he said, then muttered something she couldn't quite make out. "See anything?"

"No. Nothing." Her hand holding the gun felt sweaty. "The shooter could be hiding anywhere in the woods next to the house or across the street." The exhaustion she had felt sitting on the porch had been replaced by a buzz of adrenaline. No way she'd sleep tonight. "Where are you, Chewie?" she whispered, growing more worried for her furry friend.

"He'll show up," Harrison reassured her.

Becky shot Harrison a quick glance, then went back to peering out a corner of the window. "I hate to think someone would hurt him."

"Don't think about that."

"Hard not to. Chewie's the only one who has been by my side this whole time."

"What am I? Chopped liver?" Harrison joked, obviously trying to add levity to a tense situation.

She laughed, appreciating his efforts. Her muscles strained from staying hunched down by the window, careful to only peek out at the very bottom lower corner.

Just then a little fuzzy ball of fur emerged from the shadows and bounded up the porch steps. She fisted her hands to keep from jumping up and throwing the door open for him. She watched until she couldn't see him any longer from her position on the floor. The next moment she heard him clawing at the door. When no one answered, he started yipping. The dog wouldn't stop until she let him in.

"I have to let Chewie in."

Becky locked gazes with Harrison before crawling past the window. He got up with a groan and held out his arm. "Let me."

Her gaze dropped to the dish towel pressed to his wound. It was soaked with blood. Her stomach did a little flip-flop and she immediately felt queasy. There was a reason she wasn't a doctor, besides the exorbitant cost of higher education. Suddenly she felt a little thoughtless that she had been more worried about Chewie than the man who took a bullet for her.

She studied Harrison's face while Chewie scratched at the door. Even in the heavily shadowed room, she could see the color draining from his face. "You need to sit down." She guided him against the wall and it scared her when he didn't put up a fight as she eased him to a seated position.

He closed his eyes, seemingly resigned. "Don't make yourself a target."

"Not in my plans." She pressed her palm to his clammy forehead before rushing to the front door. Crouching low and standing against the wall, she twisted the lock and opened the door just enough to allow Chewie to slip through. Becky slammed the door shut again and turned the lock.

Becky gave Chewie a quick once-over. After assuring herself he wasn't injured, she hustled back over to Harrison, who now seemed disoriented and gray.

Becky cupped his cheek. "Ambulance is on its way. You're going to be okay. Just hold on." Her mouth went dry and she was too numb to feel anything.

And as if an answer to her prayer, she heard sirens in the distance. "You're going to be okay," she repeated. "Just hold on."

TWELVE

A buzzing sounded in Harrison's head as myriad disjointed images flashed behind his eyelids. The distant sound of an overhead paging system pulled him up through a dark tunnel to a bright light.

He opened his eyes and immediately slammed them shut. *Very* bright light. Painfully bright light. The long line of fluorescent lights burned through his eyeballs.

Where am I?

A shadow crossed his face and he tried to pry his eyes open again. This time he was rewarded with Becky's pretty but concerned smile. She spoke in a reassuring tone, "You're okay. You lost a lot of blood, so you need to relax." Her warm hand on his shoulder grounded him. "You just got out of surgery. They removed the bullet from your arm."

"Ah," he groaned. It was all coming back to him. The gunshot. Scrambling off the front porch. Hunkering down in her house. Chewie barking at the door. That was the last thing he could remember.

"How do you feel?" she asked.

"I've felt better," he said. "Did they catch the trigger-happy guy?"

"No, but the sheriff's department is looking for him."

His brain ached as he tried to figure out who might still have it out for Becky. Ned had come forward, admitting he had used excessive force when he beat Elijah. Basically, his clearing Becky's name should have taken her off the target list of any of Elijah's friends, and certainly the officers in the sheriff's department would feel less animosity toward her, knowing that Ned took responsibility for his actions.

However, those who shot at innocent people while they sat on a front porch weren't exactly rational thinkers.

And feelings died hard.

Or aren't any of these events connected? Unable to think straight, he lifted his hand to rub his eyes when he realized he was attached to an IV.

Maybe there had been developments while he was unconscious. "Does anyone have any idea who could have done this?"

"Nothing yet. Believe me, I'm going to make sure this is a top priority now that I'm back at work. The sheriff may not let me personally investigate this one, but I'll be in his face every day. Demanding updates." If Harrison wasn't loopy on pain meds, he might suspect Becky was upset. *Very upset.*

"Are you okay?" he asked, his voice hoarse.

Becky turned and dragged a hand through her ponytail. He studied her profile until she finally turned back to him, biting her lip. "You shouldn't have dived in front of me."

He reached out to touch her hand resting on the side rail, when she pulled it back slightly, causing him to miss. His fingertips brushed hers, but his arm felt too heavy to try again. He wanted to tell her that he wouldn't have been able to look at himself in the mirror if she had been hurt because he couldn't protect her.

Like he hadn't protected his brother. But his mind was too foggy to explain all that to her, at least coherently, without sounding like a lovesick fool.

Is that what I am? I hardly know her.

He pushed up on one elbow and grimaced.

Becky placed her hand on his shoulder. "Don't strain."

"Water, please." His eyes moved to the pitcher on the bedside table. Becky picked up the cup and held the straw to his lips. The water felt cool going down his throat. "It's not safe for you to be alone." Even as he said the words, he knew they didn't sound right. She was a sheriff's deputy.

He closed his eyes briefly and bit back his frustration. He wanted to be back on his feet so he could protect Becky.

"I'll be fine. You know I'm not helpless."

He knew, but he didn't like it. "When do I get out of here?"

"You'll have to wait until the physician comes in. They wouldn't tell me much. Privacy laws and everything."

Harrison plucked at the ribbon on his hospital gown at his neck. "Where are my clothes? We need to get out of here."

"You're not going anywhere until the doctor releases you." She patted his chest in a familiar gesture he was growing to like. "Blood ruined your shirt. Maybe I can run by your house and pick up fresh clothes so you have something to wear when you do get released?" She sounded a little bit like she was appeasing him.

"I don't want you driving to my house alone."

"Are you afraid I'll riffle through your sock drawer?" She laughed. He liked it. She didn't do it nearly enough.

"It's not—"

"I know what it is. But I'm a deputy. I can protect myself."

He tried to let the reality of that settle in, but his thoughts were hazy.

She cocked her head and seemed to be studying his face. "If we're going to be friends, you're going to have to get used to that idea. You're not going to go on patrol with me, are you? Protect me from all the bad guys?" Her pink lips twitched before she drew in a deep breath. "Don't treat me like I'm helpless." She leaned in and whispered, "This is exactly part of the reason I refuse to get involved with a fellow officer. There's that whole chivalrous thing going on. Then it gets…complicated."

"That's not what this is about. Someone's out to get you. They shot at you while we were sitting on the porch."

"They shot at *us*," she said evenly.

"I don't recall having made any enemies in Quail Hollow," Harrison said.

"Our jobs make us targets. I have been trained to protect myself." She walked around to the other side of his bed and picked up a plastic bag on the chair. "Are your house keys in your pants pocket?"

"Should be," he said, letting his head sink back into his pillow and fighting a battle against his drooping eyelids.

He heard a jangling as her shadow crossed his line of vision behind closed eyelids. "I'll grab your clean clothes. Will I find them in your closet? A dresser?"

"Folded. Top of dryer. Laundry room off the kitchen," he said, realizing despite his protests she was going to leave and get him clean clothes. The only consolation was that he might get out of here faster.

"Why doesn't that surprise me?"

"At least they're clean *and* folded." He laughed, then yawned.

She patted his chest again. "Sleep. I'll be right back. Maybe you'll have word from the doctor by then."

"Okay." Next thing he knew he was drifting off to sleep. He hadn't even remembered Becky slipping out the door. A rapping sounded on the door frame of the semiprivate room in recovery. He opened his eyes to find the sheriff standing there, hat in hand.

He blinked against the light, confused and disappointed that this was the face greeting him and not Becky.

"You caused some excitement around Deputy Spoth's place."

"Is she here?"

The sheriff glanced around the room. "No, I haven't seen her."

Harrison felt for the bed controls and raised the head of the bed so he could sit up and get a better read on the man he didn't fully trust, not after he lied—or technically omitted—that his nephew was one of the men shooting targets behind Becky's house.

The only people who kept secrets were those who had something to hide. And Harrison didn't like it one bit that someone had been targeting her house again today. A part of him wondered if he had dropped the ball by not pursuing the tip on the sheriff's nephew days ago. But Ned's confession and Becky's reinstatement made following up seem less urgent. Had he been wrong?

"Did they find anyone?" Harrison sniffed, trying to ignore the pain pulsing through his arm where the bullet had ripped through. Absentmindedly, he touched the bandage, wondering when the doctor would be in here to give him a full report. He needed to get out of here.

"Not yet, but they're canvassing the woods." The sheriff's expression didn't give anything away.

"Think you should run another check on the four guys who were doing target practice last week behind Becky's house? See if all of them are accounted for?"

A subtle flinch skittered across the sheriff's face. So subtle that Harrison would have missed it if he hadn't been studying his superior.

The weight of her gun on her hip provided a sense of security as Becky strode out the emergency room exit of the hospital while keeping her focus on her surroundings. Fortunately, hospital security had allowed her to keep her weapon. She had lost track of time and was surprised by how dark it was.

Of course, it was close to ten o'clock at night.

Fortunately, the parking lot was brightly lit and a security guard was stationed at the entrance to the ER.

Becky rolled back her shoulders, surprised at how stiff she had been holding her posture while she was waiting for Harrison to wake up after surgery.

Thank you, Lord, for watching over him.

They had only known each other for a short time

and she hadn't allowed herself to process the jumble of emotions she was feeling. She couldn't deny they had grown close. Closer than she realized until the thought of him not waking up made her feel empty inside.

She didn't know what to do with these feelings. Perhaps their bond had been made stronger because the two of them had very few people to rely on, other than each other.

She had a tough time reconciling her emotions. She had always seen herself as single. Independent. Not leaning on anyone. Wasn't that the point of leaving the Amish?

Was it?

She glanced both ways as she stepped off the sidewalk and crossed the parking lot between two parked cars. She couldn't stop thinking about how devastated she would have been if the gunman had killed Harrison. Or were her emotions born out of relief, pure and simple, that he hadn't died on her account? It wasn't like she had tons of experience dating. Paul King had been her only suitor when she was still Amish, and back then, it was like following a prescribed script.

Could she and Harrison have a future? Not likely if he was going back to Buffalo at some point.

Shoving aside the distracting thoughts, Becky held out her key fob and unlocked the door to her car. She surveyed the area to make sure no one was around before climbing behind the steering wheel.

As she pulled out onto the road, her car felt a bit sluggish, but it wasn't like she was driving a brand new vehicle. She glanced down at Harrison's address again.

She picked up the piece of paper and a loud, clunky sound made her stomach drop. "Oh no," she muttered as she clutched the steering wheel with both hands, crumbling the paper. The entire vehicle rumbled beneath her and she had a hard time steering.

She scanned the road around her, grateful there were no other cars around. The car sputtered and putt-putted until she had to pull over on the side of the road.

Groaning, she pushed open the door. She reached down and released the hood. She climbed out and walked around to the front. Steam poured from under the hood. As much as she knew about caring for a horse and making sure he didn't get overworked, she knew next to nothing about cars. But she did have roadside service and a cell phone. Better to call them than get burned by the steam.

She walked around to the passenger side, opened the door and grabbed her cell phone from the passenger seat. Just then, a pickup truck pulled in behind her. A young man with a baseball cap tugged down low climbed out. "Got a flat?" Something about the lack of emotion in his tone made her skin crawl.

She watched him cautiously, feeling the weight of her gun on her hip, hidden by her T-shirt. Something about him set off alarm bells. However, by all accounts, he was just a good Samaritan, offering help. But out on the deserted country road, alone, at night, was enough for her to exercise caution.

"No, I broke down." She waved him off. "I have roadside assistance. I'll be fine. I already called them," she lied, as a matter of self-preservation. She didn't want the stranger to know how truly vulnerable she was.

"I hate to leave a little lady like you out here on the side of the road all alone at night. I'll wait with you."

"No need." Her stomach quivered. She let her hand slide over the butt of her gun and her fingers twitched. Even though her instincts were screaming to pull out her gun and point it at him to protect herself, she was suddenly doubting herself.

Doubting all her training.

Tomorrow she would finally have her job back as a deputy and she couldn't risk a run-in tonight that might make the news.

Off-duty deputy shoots good Samaritan.

But if she let her guard down and something bad happened, she'd make the evening news, too, but for far more permanent reasons.

"Didn't catch your name?" She tried to sound casual.

"Don't believe I gave it." A corner of his mouth twitched in the moonlight.

The *clip clop clip* of a horse coming over the hill caught her attention. Based on the shift in body language, it had caught the young man's, too.

The Amish man in the wagon pulled back on his reins. Becky's heart slowed to a dull *whoosh-whoosh-whoosh* when she recognized her married brother.

Thank God.

"Hello, Levi." A long time ago they had been close. Now, because she had left the Amish, she had only seen his wife and two young kids from a distance. While out and about in town, they had silently greeted each other with a subtle head nod. Maybe someday they'd be allowed to be closer. When more time had passed.

"Ah, Rebecca. Your fancy car isn't quite so reliable." His eyes were heavily shadowed by the brim of his hat and she couldn't tell if he was joking or not. He liked to tease her when they were growing up. At the time, it frustrated Becky, but what she'd give now to go back to a simpler time when he was razzing her about how her pie wasn't as good as their *mem's*.

"I'm afraid my car's *not* very reliable." She wondered if her brother could feel the tension. Would he understand the edginess radiating off her wasn't due to their estranged relationship?

The man who had stopped to help her came up behind her. She was angry at herself for letting her brother distract her. For allowing the stranger to approach her from behind.

"Do you need help?" her brother asked.

"No, we're fine," the man said as he stood a fraction too close, pressing something hard into her side.

"Um…" A tingling started in her fingertips and raced up her arms.

The man whispered, "I have a gun. If you don't want your Amish friend hurt, tell him to leave."

"Are you sure?" her brother asked again. "I can drop you off at home."

"No, no, it's fine." She fought to keep the panic out of her voice. "You better hurry home to your family. I'll be fine."

Her brother seemed to stare at her for a long moment before flicking the reins. "Come on, Brownie."

Becky nearly cried at the sound of her former horse's name. She waved and forced a bright smile, if for no other reason than to protect her brother. She refused to bring any more grief into her family's lives.

As the sound from the horse's hooves grew more distant, she lifted her hand slightly, an attempt to grab her own gun. But the man was a step ahead. He snatched her wrist and twisted her arm up behind her. His hat tumbled off in the tussle and landed at her feet. Pain radiated through her shoulder and back. Before she had a chance to spin around and free herself, he pressed a gun into her side. Then handcuffed her wrists.

"I know what you're capable of. This time, instead of me getting a bloody nose, you'll get a bullet in your side."

Becky tugged on her handcuffs and bit back her frustration. The parking garage in Buffalo.

This man had attacked her, but she had been much quicker at defending herself. Her brother's arrival, his offer of help, had actually made her vulnerable. Her attacker wasn't going to be thwarted so easily a second time.

Now she was at his mercy.

"What do you want?" she asked, hiking up her chin, refusing to let him see her fear.

"What do I want?" he said in a mocking tone.

She jerked away from his grasp and spun around. Despite having her hands bound, she got up in his face. "I'm not going with you." Her pulse roared in her ears. And that was when she recognized him. A flush of dread washed over her and the ground swayed.

He lifted the gun to her forehead. "I've got nothing to lose. Try me." The dead look in his eyes drove his point home.

"Okay. I'll go with you. Don't hurt me." She had to buy time. She had her cell phone in her back pocket. Maybe he'd forget. Maybe he wouldn't pay attention long enough for her to text Harrison. Tell him who her harasser was.

But why was he doing this to her?

He took her gun and shoved it in his waistband. His fingers dug into her forearm as he forced her around to the back of his truck. He opened the tailgate and made her climb in under the canvas stretched across the bed. "Try anything stupid and I'll kill you."

She swallowed around a too-tight throat and nodded briefly. She lifted one leg and put her knee on the tailgate and hesitated. Hopping up while her hands were handcuffed behind her back posed an additional challenge. The sound of a car approaching made him shove her inside quickly and he slammed the tailgate, sealing her between the hard metal of the truck and the soft canvas of the bedcover.

She listened hard. His footsteps crunched on the gravel. He opened the door. Slammed the door. The engine started.

Her arms ached as she slid her cell phone from her back pocket. On the bed of the truck, she twisted awkwardly to see the screen. She was grateful for backlit screens. With trembling fingers, she texted the most important thing first:

Lucas Handler.

Send.

Kidnapped. Blue Truck. GMC.

Send. Send. Send.

Each message she got off was a small victory. Breadcrumbs leading to her location.

The truck slowed and Becky rolled back on her

elbow, painful bone-to-metal contact. The engine still purred. Car door slammed. Heavy footsteps. Running.

The cell phone grew slippery in her sweat-slicked hands.

The tailgate flew open. She tried to hide the phone under her shirt, but with her hands bound, she was too slow. He ripped the phone from her hand and threw it across the road.

Had he noticed what she had done?

Lucas Handler, one of the young men conducting target practice behind her house had kidnapped her. And now Deputy Harrison James knew.

She prayed.

"I don't think we need to worry about those young men. I checked them out personally. They're good kids," the sheriff said, rubbing a hand across his jaw.

Harrison gritted his teeth, trying to contain his growing anger and wishing he had full use of his left arm. "And you know this because one of them is your nephew."

The sheriff jerked back his head. "How did you…?" Letting his question trail off, he seemed to change his approach midsentence. "That has nothing to do with anything."

"Why didn't you tell me Tyler Flint was your nephew the minute I showed you his identification? The absence of transparency—" he spit the sheriff's favorite word back at him "—makes me think either you or Tyler has something to hide."

The sheriff seemed to slump as he took a step back and then lowered himself into the hard plastic chair. "My nephew's a good kid. Just impulsive. My sister sent him to live with me. Straighten him out. He's got a scholarship to college next fall if he can keep his nose clean his senior year."

"You interfered with an investigation so your nephew wouldn't get into trouble?" Anger pulsed through Harrison, making him sharper despite the meds in his system. All the color seemed to drain from the sheriff's face. "What else haven't you told us?"

The sheriff ran a hand over his short haircut. "Nothing. Nothing at all."

Harrison hated that he was stuck in this hospital bed when all he wanted to do was rip the IV out of his arm and… *Grrr…* "You let politics get in the way."

The sheriff squared his shoulders and looked every bit like the man running for office. "There is no indication my nephew did anything. There was no need to stir up trouble."

"Your omission makes me wonder what else you're not telling me."

A muscle ticked in the sheriff's jaw.

A ding sounded from the plastic bag hanging over the hook at the back of the door. Worried that it might be Becky, he pointed at it. "Get my phone."

The sheriff shot him a glance, probably surprised his subordinate didn't say please. However, considering their exchange, he no doubt realized he better do what Harrison had asked. *Now.* The sheriff stood, grabbed the bag and tossed it into Harrison's lap.

With one hand, Harrison found his folded up jeans and dug out his cell phone. He glanced at the display. He squinted at the screen, trying to figure out what Becky meant by "Lucas Handler."

Then the words that came through next send terror pressing into his heart: Kidnapped. Blue truck. GMC.

The roaring in his ears drowned out all the other sounds in the small recovery room. He swiped his hand across the screen and pressed call. The phone rang and went to voice mail.

"Call me."

"What's going on?" the sheriff asked.

"Becky just texted me. Now I can't reach her." Harrison called the number again and waited. Again, her voice mail.

Harrison didn't like this one bit. He flipped back the thin white hospital bedspread and gritted his teeth when pain shot through his arm. He hesitated a fraction of a moment before sliding the IV out of his hand. He gave the raw flesh on the back of his hand a quick glance before swinging his feet over the edge of the bed.

"Whoa, whoa. I don't think you're supposed to get up." The sheriff held up his hands as if he was going to try to stop him. *Not likely.*

"Not only am I leaving, but you're driving me."

THIRTEEN

Every body part that came into contact with the steel bed of the pickup truck ached as the crazed driver made sharp turns and hit ruts. Becky would probably be black-and-blue all over tomorrow; that is, *if* she lived to see the sunrise.

No, she'd live. She *had* to.

She bit back a yelp as the truck turned, apparently off the smooth main road and onto a side road, maybe a driveway. The vehicle bobbled over each and every rut. Where was he taking her? She wished he had stuffed her in the backseat and not the back of the pickup, then maybe she'd have a chance to talk him out of this. As it stood, she just had that much longer to imagine her fate.

"You'll be fine," she whispered to herself. The sound of her voice calmed her. "You're a trained sheriff's deputy." She drew in a deep breath as the truck came to a sudden stop and she banged her head on the bump out from the wheel well. She yanked on her wrists, hoping against hope that the handcuffs had come loose.

She tried to stretch her legs in the cramped space but it was of no use. She'd have to comply with his commands until she got her feet under her and her hands free.

She found herself holding her breath. Listening.

Car door slammed.

Footsteps. Growing fainter.

What does that mean? Is he leaving me here?

A trickle of sweat trailed down her forehead and into her ear. She wasn't sure what terrified her more: being left trapped in the truck breathing in the stale smell of vinyl mixed with soil or being dragged out to some unknown fate.

A bubble of panic welled up and threatened to consume her.

Stay calm. You'll be fine. She pressed her eyes shut and did something she should have done immediately. *Dear Lord, protect me. Keep me clearheaded. Let me see the way out.*

Taking calming breaths, she listened harder. The sound of a car passing. Fast. They weren't too far off the main road.

Footsteps again.

The tailgate creaked as he lowered it. Fresh air and moonlight flooded the space. Becky did her best to act calm. Keep this kid calm.

"Where are we?" she asked, trying to take in as much as she could as he gripped her forearm and yanked her out of the truck. Unable to get her feet under her fast enough, she fell to her knees.

Annoyed, Lucas wrenched her to her feet. "Hurry up." He glanced around as if he feared someone was about to find them.

She prayed that meant they weren't in a remote location.

Nothing struck Becky as unique. Trees, country road, small house hunkered in the shadows. Nothing to pinpoint her location. "Is this your house?" She avoided calling him by his name. That was her secret. She feared his reaction if he realized she knew his identity.

When he didn't answer, she asked again. "Do you live here?"

"No, but someone I want you to see does," the kid said, surprising her with an answer of any kind.

"Are they home?"

"He's supposed to be, but he didn't answer the door." He sounded genuinely disappointed.

"Do you know who I am? I'm a sheriff's deputy. You'll be in a lot of trouble for kidnapping a law-enforcement officer."

The kid scoffed. "If you were much of a deputy, you wouldn't be so easily kidnapped."

"How'd that work out for you in the parking garage? Nose still hurt?" She took a shot at his self-confidence. He seemed to be deflated after learning no one was home. Had he kidnapped her on a dare? Wanted to show someone what he had done?

He glared at her for a long minute before his expression shifted. "You won't catch me off guard again." He tugged on the handcuffs and pain ripped through her raw wrists. "Now look who has the upper hand."

"People will be looking for me."

"Maybe." He seemed disinterested. "But will they find you in time?"

He pushed her up two steps to the front porch. Their footfalls sounded loud on the wood slats as if they were the only people around for miles. Keys jangled and he pushed past her to unlock the door.

He grabbed her forearm and shoved her inside. The place smelled closed up. Like someone had been away for a few days, at least. Lucas went to the keypad and entered the alarm code.

"Who lives here?"

"Shut up." He shoved her and she bumped against the hall table. A collection of photos fell over like dominos. Behind her, the kid flipped on a light. A photo of Ned Reich stared back at her. He was standing with a woman, a little boy next to him. The portrait of a happy family.

A flush of dread washed over her. She willed herself to be calm. "This is Ned Reich's home. How do you know Ned?" Her entire scalp tingled and she struggled to swallow.

Lucas flinched, but he set his jaw and glared at her, remaining silent.

She tried again. "Who is this little boy in the photo? You?"

"Shut up." Lucas's expression was hard. Angry. "Do I look like that snot-nosed kid?"

"Why are we in Deputy Reich's house? That's where we are, right?" Was this some form of retribution toward her and Deputy Reich for their involvement in the Elijah Lapp incident? Or had he brought her here as punishment for her role in Reich's suspension? The pieces didn't quite fit.

She studied his face. The dead look in his eyes made icy dread pool in her stomach.

He grabbed her by the arm again and shoved her into the family room at the back of the house. A kitchen was visible on the other end. It was what she heard her Realtor call an open concept. All the ways *Englischers* lived baffled her when she first left the Amish. The Amish had clean, well-maintained homes, but all these extras were perplexing to her, even now.

She had to lean back on her hands because of the handcuffs. She shifted, trying to find a comfortable position. Lucas paced in front of her as if he had miscalculated something. His growing agitation was rubbing off on her. Making her skin buzz. She needed him to be calm. *She* needed to be calm.

"You should have never been made a deputy. You're not competent." He pivoted and turned back around. He plowed a shaky hand through his straggly hair.

"What did I ever do to you?" The words flew from her lips before she could call them back.

"You took my job." He kicked a stuffed animal that got in his way. Becky imagined a well-loved pet lived somewhere in this house.

She studied him carefully, realizing there was no rationalizing with an irrational person. She couldn't have taken his job any more than Harrison had taken his job. After all, Harrison had been hired after her. But for some reason he had focused on her as the guilty party. Why? Because she was an outsider? A woman? Because she had drawn his attention with all the news coverage of the beating of Elijah Lapp? Had he targeted her because he felt she was a symbol of everything that he felt was wrong with the system? Was he on a mission to hurt Deputy Reich, too?

After leaving the Amish, Becky had immersed herself in newspaper and online articles about the world around her. A world she had been living in, but hadn't been a part of. Initially, she had her doubts. Wondered if she made the right decision. The evil around her made her fantasize about running back to the insular world of her family. But God's calling to live a different life had been louder than the whispers of uncertainty buzzing in her ears as she tried to fall asleep each night those first few lonely months.

Now after all that, is this where I'm meant to die?

She couldn't accept that. She wouldn't. God hadn't placed her on this difficult journey to have it end here.

"Are you mad at me because of the incident with Deputy Reich?" She kept her tone soft, inquisitive.

The man's fingers flicked and closed, flicked and closed as he paced in front of her. He was growing more agitated, leading her to believe she was on the right track.

"Are you looking to get back at Deputy Reich and me for hurting Elijah? Are you and Elijah friends?"

He squinted at her. His mouth was twisted in a mocking grin. "You'd make a crummy detective."

She stared at him a long minute. "Is Deputy Reich a mentor of yours?"

The man spun around and bent down and picked up one end of the coffee table. Candles, decorations and TV remotes crashed to the floor. She recoiled at the uncontrolled anger pulsing off him.

"He is my father. He is my father. My *father*." His face grew red and spittle flew from his lips.

Becky blinked slowly, trying to let that register. This man was Ned Reich's son. This man was out for revenge against her *because of* his father.

She tugged at her handcuffs and feared the desperateness of the situation, but she forced herself to remain calm. Words came to her. "Then you know your father is a good man who made a mistake. He wouldn't want you to hurt me."

A muscle worked in his jaw. "How do you know what he'd want? You ruined his life." Lucas breathed in and out quickly through his flaring nose. His eyes darted around the room as if he was replaying her words in his mind. "A mistake? The only mistake he made was confessing. He needed to stay strong. Fight the charges."

"He's sorry. He told me as much."

"We're only sorry you testified against him."

"With or without my testimony, he couldn't explain away what happened in the video."

"You made everything worse." He glared at her and for a fraction of a moment, she thought he was going to charge at her. Instinctively, her stomach clenched. She didn't have her hands free to defend herself.

"Hurting me won't solve anything."

It was his turn to blink at her, processing her words. "If you hadn't responded to the call with your dash cam rolling, his life wouldn't have been ruined. If you hadn't been a witness against him. If you hadn't…" His voice bellowed in the confines of his father's house.

Becky opened her mouth to protest, but the rage flaring in his nostrils gave her pause.

"His life is ruined because of you."

Harrison jumped out of the patrol car the second it stopped in front of the address on Lucas Handler's driver's license. Holding his injured arm close to his side, he ran to the front door of a trailer with rust running down its white sides. The door swung open as if someone had been waiting for them.

"I'm looking for Lucas Handler."

The woman's eyes grew dark. "What's he done now?"

"Is he your son?" Harrison asked, trying to tamp down his frustration. The woman looked past him to the sheriff standing outside his patrol car. They had already called in Becky as missing. Possibly kidnapped. Other patrols were out looking for her. Harrison wouldn't rest easy until she was found.

"Who's asking?" The woman's gaze dropped to his arm in a sling. He had somehow managed to throw on his bloodied and torn shirt.

"I'm Deputy James." He touched his injured arm. "I had a little accident and I need to find your son."

She sighed heavily as if resigned to answering. "I don't know where he is."

"Has Lucas ever mentioned a Deputy Rebecca Spoth to you?"

The woman's thin eyebrows rose under her long bangs. "Is that what this is about? That Amish woman who thinks she can be a cop?" She crossed her arms tightly across her thin frame. A smug expression slanted her mouth. "She doesn't know her place."

Harrison clenched his jaw, knowing if he responded how he wanted to respond she'd shut down. And right now he needed to find Lucas.

And Becky.

"Do you know where Lucas might be?"

She shrugged. "Doesn't report in to me. Comes and goes as he pleases." She shook her head as if she never had any control over her son.

"How about Lucas's father? Could we talk to him?"

"His father's not in the picture. Never has been." The woman stared at him defiantly. She hiked her chin at the sheriff. "Why don't you ask the sheriff over there. He knows where Ned is."

"Ned?" Harrison's pulse roared in his ears. "Ned Reich?"

The woman gave him a self-satisfied smile. "Ned doesn't have anything to do with me or Lucas. I couldn't care less, but Lucas would do anything for his father. Not that his father would have anything to do with him. Rarely has. Stopped coming around as soon as he knew I was pregnant. The guy has a problem. Cheated with me on his first wife when his oldest son—Colin, he's also one of yours—was just a young boy. Swore he couldn't leave his wife until he found the next one. I heard he has himself another wife and boy. Apparently, we weren't good enough."

Harrison tried to be patient as the woman unraveled her unfortunate life story. "Has Lucas been in contact with Ned recently?"

"I don't know how Lucas spends his time. I'm not sure how to be clearer on that."

Harrison opened his wallet and pulled out his business card. He offered it to the woman, who took it reluctantly. "Call me if you see Lucas. It's important."

Harrison spun around and jogged over to the sheriff. "Did you know Lucas Handler is Ned Reich's son?"

The sheriff shook his head. "Can't say I was privy to that information."

"But your nephew is friends with him?"

The sheriff waved his hand in dismissal. "Kids just hang out. Doesn't mean they're best friends."

"Call Ned. Find out if he's with Lucas. Don't tell him what's going on." The sheriff did what Harrison asked even though the expression on his face suggested he wanted to do anything but.

Harrison still couldn't shake the feeling that the sheriff was hiding something.

He paced next to the patrol car while the sheriff made the phone call. A teenager around fifteen on a brown bike with motocross stickers plastered on the frame skidded to a stop on the gravel. "Are you here to arrest Lucas?"

Harrison studied the teen. "No, we're here to talk to him. Do you know Lucas?"

The kid roughly rubbed his nose. A large scab covered his elbow. "Everyone knows Lucas." The kid rolled his eyes. "But no one likes him."

"Why's that?"

"He's always mad. Going on about how he's going to become a deputy and come back and put us all in jail. He acts like he never did the stuff we do." The kid glanced around, acting skittish. "Nothing bad, just stuff like skidding on the gravel in front of his trailer. Playing our music loud. He once stole my friend's baseball mitt when he put it down to run in for a drink. Claims he never saw it." He shook his head in disgust.

"Any idea where Lucas hangs out?" Harrison asked.

"Mostly he hangs on the porch yelling at us. If he's not here, I don't want to know where he is."

"Thanks," Harrison said, then turned to the sheriff. "Find anything out?"

"Ned says he doesn't have much contact with his son. The son was the result of a stupid fling." The sheriff frowned. "His words, not mine. Never married the mother. The relationship has always been strained." This pretty much matched what Harrison got from the mother.

Harrison ran a hand across his jaw. "Okay, so he's not with Ned. Wonder—"

The sheriff held up his hand. "Ned's out of town. Gone fishing up at Lake George. Just turned on his phone—was trying to go off the grid for a bit, but knew with everything going on regarding his employment that he better not go completely silent. Anyway, he had a notice on his home monitoring app. Someone entered his house here in town. Knew the alarm code."

"Couldn't be Lucas, right? Not if Ned doesn't have contact with his son. He wouldn't know the code," Harrison reasoned.

"Here's the thing. About a year ago Ned reached out to the kid. Thought maybe he was wrong in not being a father figure. Even had him dog-sit." The sheriff pushed up his hat. "But the dog wasn't well cared for and the two had a blowout. Haven't spoken much since."

"So, unless Ned changed the code, Lucas has it."

"Exactly. Ned never changed it." The sheriff reached for the car door handle. "Told Ned we'd check on his property. Told him not to call the house. We want the element of surprise."

Harrison pulled the passenger door open. "What are we waiting for?"

Becky studied Lucas from her seat in the corner of the couch. He opened and closed closets and drawers with short, jerky movements. She wondered if he was under the influence of something. His distraction never lasted long enough for her to make a move, especially with her hands in cuffs.

A few feet in front of her, Lucas opened the cabinet under the TV then froze as if he had remembered something. He slowly pivoted, glared at her with a distant expression, stood and then strode over to the door and opened it. Watching carefully, she slid to the front of the couch cushion and shifted her weight to her feet. Ready to pounce.

Lucas slammed the door. "His car's not here. I thought I heard it. I think he went fishing." A muscle worked in his jaw as his gaze locked on hers. He tilted his head and studied her, perhaps trying to read her thoughts, trying to figure out why she had positioned herself forward on the couch. Was he going to lash out at her? Make her regret her feeble attempt at overpowering him.

She slid back onto the couch casually. "Do you like to go fishing?"

"He only takes Noah fishing."

Becky licked her lips. "Is Noah the little boy in the photographs?"

Lucas practically snarled. "My half brother, not that anyone would know it."

"Maybe your father would take you fishing if you asked him to." Lucas seemed like someone who would be too proud to ask for what he wanted.

Lucas plowed a hand through his hair. "I need to see him. Show him what I've done for him."

"What have you done for him?" Her pulse whooshed loudly in her ears as she held her breath, waiting for the answer. Fearing the answer.

"I'm going to take care of his biggest problem." His

expression was a mix of determination and anger. "He's finally going to be proud of me."

Becky slid forward on the couch cushion again, her heart jackhammering in her chest. "Hurting me is not going to solve anything. Can you please remove my handcuffs? It's hard to sit like this. My arms are aching."

He stopped and stared at her; his eyes looked blank, but something compelled him to grant her request. He put the handcuffs back on, but this time in front. She counted it as a victory. "Thank you," she whispered.

"Don't thank me." He couldn't seem to make eye contact. She wanted to get him talking, hoping to break down the wall around his heart.

"I can imagine you're sorry you ran me off the road and slashed my tires."

His gaze shot up to her face and he laughed. "Sorry? My only regret is that I didn't kill you when I had the chance." He made a gesture of a gun with his fingers and slowly lowered it to take aim at her head. "If my shot had been one foot lower, your brains would have been splattered all over your little dog. Don't think I'm a bad shot. The miss was intentional. Fear is a powerful motivator."

"Motivator?"

"To motivate you to leave my father alone."

Becky threaded her fingers and twisted. "Did your friends know what you were up to?" Maybe if she kept him talking she could buy some time. She wasn't sure at all if Harrison would figure out where they were. They had no idea Lucas was Ned's son.

An ugly smile pulled at his lips. "My friends?"

"Yes, Deputy James talked to four young men, including you, the day you almost shot me. The day you and your friends were having target practice behind my house." She watched as he scratched his neck viscously as if a mosquito had bitten him. "Did your friends know what you were up to? Were they in on it?" She wasn't sure why she was asking him, but the longer he answered questions, the less likely he would act on his wish to see her dead.

"They were clueless." He seemed to take pride in his proclamation. "I told them that nature called. I slid into the woods." He gave her an exaggerated frown as if he was recalling the events of that day. "I was going to shoot out a window in your house. Scare you back to the Amish farm where you came from. But imagine my surprise when you were outside." He made a shooting sound with his lips. "Bang. Bang. I waited until one of the guys took aim at a tin can, masking my shot. The bark exploded and the look of terror on your face was worth it. Hid the gun in a hollowed-out log. Went back to get it later. I'm not so stupid. Not sure why my dad is so hard on me."

Becky floated between fear of and sympathy for this truly lost young man. "You don't have to do this, Lucas. Let me go." She was going to add, "no one has to know," but it seemed rather cliché.

The doorbell rang.

Lucas swung his attention toward the front door and cursed under his breath. They both knew his father wouldn't ring the doorbell. Lucas held up his index finger to his mouth in a harsh hush gesture.

The sound of her ragged breath filled her ears. Should she yell out for help? Seconds ticked by, indecision weighing on her. She couldn't risk the safety of whoever was at the door.

The doorbell chimed again followed by a pounding.

"Lucas Handler, it's the sheriff. Open up."

"What the…?" Lucas darted over to the kitchen and grabbed her gun from the counter. Becky cringed at how carelessly he handled the weapon. Hated that it was her weapon he was going to use against the sheriff.

With a determined set of the jaw, Lucas stomped over to the couch and yanked Becky up by the front of her shirt. Her awkward forward momentum caused her shoulder to crash into his solid chest.

"Lucas," the sheriff yelled again, "we know you're in there. We're looking for Deputy Spoth. Come on, son. Your dad wouldn't want this."

Lucas's face grew red with rage. "You have no idea what my father wants. You fired him."

While Lucas directed his fury toward the front of the house, out of the corner of her eye Becky thought she saw a shadow in the yard. Hope blossomed in her chest. She made sure Lucas was focused on the front door, and she turned her full attention to the glass sliders in the kitchen. Harrison peeked around the corner, careful not to make himself a target, and gave her a reassuring nod.

Becky had to think fast. They were on the precipice of a major tragedy, of which she was going to be the star. She bowed her head and tucked her face into her shoulder. "I think I'm going to be sick."

Lucas seemed to snap out of it for a moment, long enough to register what she had said.

"Please, I'm going to throw up."

Lucas gestured toward the kitchen sink. "In there. I'm not cleaning up your mess."

Becky nodded contritely and took a small step backward. She needed him to believe she was weak. A victim. At this moment she chose to be anything but.

Panicked by the sheriff at the front door, Lucas left her to move about unchecked. He jogged to the front door and positioned himself against the wall, holding the gun in both hands now, down between his legs, his attention focused on a thin, smoked-glass side light running the length of the door. She prayed the sheriff stayed clear of the window, otherwise it would be a bullet from her gun in his gut.

Becky pivoted and walked slowly, so as not to draw attention to herself. At that exact moment the sheriff started pounding again. Lucas jammed a hand through his hair, his whole body trembling. An animal trapped in a corner with no hope of escape.

Becky let out a long, shaky breath, knowing they had reached a critical point.

As she moved toward the sink, she hustled past the slider, flicked the lock in one fluid motion. Her heart dropped when she noticed a bar reinforcement. Watching Lucas out of the corner of her eye, she released the bar and it dropped with a clack.

"What's that?" Lucas yelled, marching partially down the hallway with short, jittery steps.

Becky leaned heavily on a chair. "Sorry, I tripped." Holding her breath, she watched as Lucas shifted his attention back to the front door. She moved toward the sink. Her throat growing tight, she turned on the faucet and made like she was splashing water on her face, the entire time watching the situation out of the corner of her eye.

Harrison slid open the door and aimed his gun at Lucas with his one good hand. "Drop the gun."

Lucas's eyes widened and all the color drained from his face. He seemed baffled that the sheriff was at the front door while Deputy James had made it in through the back.

Becky grabbed a cast-iron skillet off the hook in the kitchen and crept through the dining room, emerging on the other side of the foyer with a clear sight of Lucas.

"Drop the gun!" Harrison yelled again.

The young man's fingers twitched near the trigger. His arm started to rise. Becky lifted the skillet with her two cuffed hands and ran at Lucas, clobbering him over the head.

Lucas crumpled to the ground in a heap of limbs and baggy clothes. Becky dropped the pan; her arms felt like JELL-O.

She turned to look at Harrison. He slid his gun back into its holster and without one note of surprise said, "Nice job." He opened the door to the sheriff. "There's your man."

The sheriff crouched down, picked up the gun and pressed his fingers to Lucas's neck to check for a pulse. "What did you do?"

"What I had to," Becky said, pointing with her thumb at the heavy skillet on the table.

The sheriff handed keys to Harrison and he quickly undid her handcuffs. He gently ran his hand over the tender skin of her wrist. "You okay?"

She narrowed her gaze at his bloodstained shirt. "I could ask the same of you."

He touched his wounded arm. "I'll live."

"I'll call an ambulance for our friend here on the floor." The sheriff stepped outside, leaving the door open.

Becky ran a hand across her face, her wrists still sore from the handcuffs. "Honestly, I didn't know I had it in me."

"I did." Harrison pulled her into a one-armed embrace and for the first time since he had been shot on her front porch—which seemed like a lifetime ago—Becky allowed herself to take a deep breath. She rested her head on his shoulder, careful not to hurt his arm.

Harrison smiled at her. "You're one tough deputy."

"Thanks for providing a distraction so I could sneak up on him."

"My pleasure." She could hear the smile in his voice as his breath whispered across her hair.

"I think it's finally over for real. Lucas was the one harassing me, trying to get payback for his father."

Harrison stepped back and ran a tender hand down her arm. "I'm happy for you. But I'm sorry I wasn't there to protect you."

"You'll have to get used to it. I'm a deputy. Your job isn't to protect me."

He opened his mouth, but whatever he was about to say died on his lips as his gaze drifted to the door.

"Ambulance is on the way." The sheriff stood in the doorway, holding his phone. "They're going to want a full statement from you, Deputy Spoth."

"Yes, sir." But this time her statement would be the end of her problems and not the beginning.

Harrison gently took her by the hand and led her outside. She drew in a deep breath of the sweet night air. "I'm grateful God was watching over me tonight. And that He sent you."

"Me, too. I don't know what I would have done…" His words trailed off and she felt his steady gaze on her as the darkness and sounds of nature crowded in on them. "You know, you're not in this alone."

"No?" She looked up at him.

"All deputies need backup," he added breezily, as if their conversation had grown too serious.

Her quiet laugh had a shaky quality to it. "Are you offering to be my backup?"

"How about an offer of dinner instead?"

Heat warmed her cheeks. "After everything we've been through, you're asking me on a date?"

"You're not going to make this easy on me, are you?"

Feeling emboldened after everything she'd been through, Becky placed her hand on his chest and stretched up to brush a kiss across his cheek. "I'd love to go to dinner. But, let's keep it low key." Harrison didn't have plans to stick around Quail Hollow long term anyway, no sense making it more than it was.

The sound of sirens approaching filed the air. "Low key sounds perfect." He placed his hand on the small of her back. "Let's go inside before the mosquitos eat us alive."

FOURTEEN

A few days later, while back at work, Becky felt like she had never left. The one big change was that she was now on the day shift and her fellow officers no longer gave her the side eye. They no more tolerated rogue deputies than she had, but it took a few of the officers a while to realize former Deputy Ned Reich wasn't the good guy they thought he was. Even his son, Deputy Colin Reich, had offered her an apology for giving her a hard time. The entire sheriff's department wanted to move forward.

Becky hoped Ned would eventually find his way. He had admitted his temper got the best of him when it came to the beating of Elijah Lapp. Fortunately, Elijah was on the mend. Last she heard, he had moved to live with family in another Amish community. And Ned lost his job. But Becky felt deep in her heart that Ned was repentant. Perhaps he could eventually find his place in this community and rise from the ashes after he served whatever sentence he received for beating a man.

But that was his journey. Not hers.

The afternoon temperatures had still remained hotter than average for Quail Hollow, New York. Calls to the sheriff's department had thankfully been slow. As Becky crested the hill near her family's farm, she decided there were other fences she needed to mend before she'd be content to settle into her new routine.

Becky parked her patrol car along the road out of respect for her Amish family and neighbors. She called into dispatch to let them know where she was. She used the guise that she was checking on the Kings' residence after the incident with the puppies.

The hot sun beat down on her hat as she walked toward the Kings' barn. She held her shoulders back. She was done letting even a hint of shame color how she felt about her job as a sheriff's deputy. Her Amish family may not like it, but there was an element of pride for serving as a law enforcement officer. Despite their tenet of staying separate, even the Amish had to admit law enforcement had the entire community's best interests at heart.

As she approached the barn, she had a sense of déjà vu, yet it felt like a million years since she had rescued Chewie from his horrible living conditions.

Oh man, Chewie, she thought. The little guy had been a great companion. She supposed she had to ask Mag if she was expecting him to come live with her. Becky had promised her sister, but she would hate to see the little fur ball go. He was her only steady companion after she and Harrison decided to keep things platonic after their dinner date.

Becky supposed it was probably for the best. Despite her growing feelings for him, they both had different paths in life. She suspected he'd be returning to Buffalo soon anyway.

Out of the corner of her eye, she noticed someone running across the yard: her old friend, Mary Elizabeth.

"Becky, is something wrong?" Mary asked.

Becky shook her head. "No. I wanted to see how things were going."

"Fine," Mary responded stiffly. "Anything else?" Mary glanced toward the barn, perhaps a bit nervously, probably wishing Becky'd leave. Her friend had been terrified she'd lose her husband if he was arrested for mistreating the dogs. But that had been resolved with fines and the promise to not mistreat animals again. Becky wanted to believe the Kings had never meant to hurt the animals, but had quickly become overwhelmed with their puppy selling enterprise.

"I don't mean to cause any trouble for you. Please, if you ever need anything from outside the Amish community, consider me a friend."

Mary bowed her head briefly, then looked back up. "I'd like that." Her cheeks reddened as if her desire didn't match what the strict rules allowed. In her heart, Becky cheered the small victories. Their friendship could never be what it was, but maybe they could stop and chat at the market when their paths crossed. Becky would learn the names of her children. Maybe help the next generation know it's okay to reach out if they need help from an *Englischer*.

"Is Paul in the barn?" Becky asked, feeling like the silence had stretched into awkward territory.

"Yah." A line marred the flawless skin of her forehead.

"I'm just going to say hello." Becky gave her old friend a quick nod, then strode toward the barn before she tried to stop her. Becky found Paul brushing a horse. He paused, looked at her with an even expression, then went back to his task.

Becky glanced around the barn. Gone was the cage holding the dogs. The space was tidy. The horses seemed well cared for. "How are you, Paul?"

"Fine." His eyes shifted skeptically. "Spying on me to see if I've broken your rules?"

Becky didn't answer, knowing he wouldn't take kindly to her patronizing him. "At lot has gone on in the community these past few weeks. Law enforcement and the Amish stay separate, but with the beating of Elijah Lapp and the intertwining of our families, that hasn't been possible." She took off her hat and touched her braids that were neatly pinned on top of her head. "I hope despite our past, there are no hard feelings. If there is anything I can ever do for your family, please let me know." Part of her hope for being a deputy and staying in Quail Hollow was to bridge the gap between the two worlds. A difficult task, for sure, but a necessary one.

"Yah." Paul's mouth twitched as if he wanted to say more, but he turned and went back to brushing the horse in silence. She'd have to take what she could get.

"Have a good afternoon." She spun on the heel of her boot and decided it was time to face her family because that was the fence she truly wanted to mend.

Becky cut through the path connecting the neighboring properties. When she was about thirty feet from her parents' house, a cute little white fur ball ran across the yard to greet her. Becky bent down and patted his head. "Well, hello there. Who are you?"

She straightened and glanced around. Mag came running out of the barn and stopped short when she saw her big sister playing with the dog. "Yours?" Becky asked.

"*Yah!* Can you believe *Dat* let me get him?" She glanced around and lowered her voice. "Sometimes I even sneak him into my room." Her parents had always believed animals belonged outside or in the barn.

"Does that mean you don't want Chewie?"

Mag's eyes widened. "I thought you loved him."

"I do." Becky couldn't contain her smile.

Mag's expression relaxed. "Well, *gut*, because now we both have dogs we love."

Becky was pleased that the dog situation had been easily resolved.

"Are *Mem* and *Dat* around?"

"In the house." Mag's gaze drifted to their well-maintained, nondescript home. A row of pale blue and gray dresses flapped in the wind on the clothesline. A sense of loss pinged her heart.

Will I ever get past the feelings of loss?

"And Abram?" Becky asked, forcing a cheeriness into her tone.

"He went to a cattle auction. Should be home later tonight." After hesitating a moment Mag said, "Come on in."

Words never sounded so sweet, but Becky wasn't naive enough to believe her parents, especially her *dat*, would feel the same way.

Mag led the way, the folds of her gown flapping against her legs. They found their parents in the kitchen. *Mem* at the stove. *Dat* at the table working on the reel of his fishing rod.

The sight, the familiar sounds, the fragrant smells,

were like a punch to Becky's gut. She hadn't realized how much she missed family until she was back in the heart of her home.

Former home.

They both looked up at their daughters at the same time. Curiosity lit her mother's expression. Stoicism defined his.

"Hello," Becky said, feeling very much like the eighteen-year-old Amish girl who had left in the middle of the night. "Um…I got my job back."

Her father ran his hand down his unkempt beard. "I can see that," he said, indicating her crisp uniform. Even though they didn't discuss it, she suspected they experienced their share of shame over the news stories suggesting Becky had beat an Amish boy and for that, she was sorry. But she was even more sorry that their estrangement meant she hadn't had her family to rely on during the lowest point in her career.

They'd never understand their daughter's career. Harrison's handsome smile came to mind. He might have been the one to stand by her side moving forward, if only his plans included staying in town. Since they didn't, she couldn't risk her heart. She had already experienced too much loss in her life.

Becky quickly shoved thoughts of Harrison aside. "I was cleared of all charges in the Elijah Lapp incident." She needed her parents to hear it from her. To know that even though their daughter left the Amish faith, she hadn't abandoned the morals that they had instilled in her.

"*Yah*, I heard. I never believed you were capable of that," her mother said. She'd probably never realize how much those words meant to her oldest daughter.

"Is that what you came here to say?" her father said, wiping off the fishing pole with a rag.

"I want you all to know I'm here if you need anything." Her words were mostly for the benefit of her little sister. She never wanted Mag to feel as alone as Becky had when she was struggling with the decision to leave the Amish.

Her father mumbled something she couldn't make out while her mother returned to stirring whatever was on the stove, leaving it up to her husband to address this weighty matter. It was this need to defer to the male that had always stuck in Becky's craw.

Speak up, Mem, *tell me how you feel!*

Just because she felt a certain way didn't mean it was the right way. The only way. Generations of Amish women had lived happily on the farm as if no time had passed. However, Becky knew it wasn't the way she wanted to live.

"Well…" Becky fidgeted with the hat in her hands. "I better get back on patrol."

"*Denki* for stopping by," her mother said as if grasping for something to say.

"You're welcome. I look forward to seeing you around town." Becky would respect her parents' wishes that they remain separate and she wouldn't continue to stop by, especially since it seemed to make them uncomfortable.

"Our worry has always been for your sister," her father said, his voice low and even. He never looked up from the work he was doing. "We never wanted you to be a negative influence."

"I understand." She did. She just didn't like it.

"However, I have come to the difficult conclusion that I can no more force Magdaline to stay among the Amish than I was able to force you to return." He set down the rag he was using on the table next to his fishing pole. "It would make your mother happy if you could come for dinner on occasion. You were never baptized into the Amish faith, so I feel we have some leeway there. It couldn't be a regular occurrence, mind you. But a special occasion."

Joy exploded in Becky's chest and she did everything to contain her excitement. She didn't want to scare anyone off. "That would be nice," she said in the same self-contained manner in which her father spoke.

"It would be," her mother said, clutching a dish towel to her chest, light beaming in her eyes.

"I should go," Becky said, and turned toward the door, more pleased with the results of her visit than she could have ever imagined. The invitation had been an olive branch extended by her father.

Mag saw her out. She leaned in and whispered, "Eli Hoffstetler asked to take me home after singing." Her sister seemed giddy. Becky could tell she was bursting with the news. The who's-who of dating was usually done quietly and engagements were only published weeks before a wedding. Becky was thrilled her sister shared this news with her.

"Do you like him?"

Mag nodded her head enthusiastically. "I've liked him since he tugged on my bonnet strings the first day of school when I was six years old."

Becky squeezed her sister's hand. "I'm happy for

you." It seemed her sister might find happiness among the Amish that she couldn't.

Becky walked toward her patrol car feeling a lightness she hadn't felt in ages.

Deputy Harrison James pulled his truck into a spot at the sheriff's station and climbed out. He had to get an update on his disability after getting shot in the arm. Two spots down, Becky pulled in with her patrol car. He'd be lying if he didn't admit he was happy to see her. He had purposely timed his visit with the end of her shift.

Harrison slammed his car door and called after her, determined not to let this get too awkward despite their decision to simply remain friends. "How's the day shift treating you?"

Becky slowed her pace and turned around, giving him a bright smile. He missed seeing her pretty face. "I like it. Finally get to live a normal life. Sleep when normal people sleep." If the fact she was beaming was any indication, she was right. The day shift agreed with her.

"Glad to hear it. Most of the calls seem tamer on day shift, too." He twisted his mouth and raised his eyebrows. "Mostly, anyway."

"True." She took a step backward and lifted her arm to the station where the deputies had to report before going home for the night. "Well, I better get moving, Chewie needs to be let out."

"You're a dog owner for the long haul?"

"Go figure." She shrugged, but he could tell she was happy about it.

"Have a good evening." She waved her hand casually, then turned to walk into the station.

He hustled to catch up to her. "I wanted to let you know I'm headed to Buffalo."

"Oh." Was that disappointment settling in the fine lines around her eyes?

"It's time I faced my past," he admitted. Long past time. He patted his arm. "Seems like a good time, considering my arm will take a bit to heal."

Becky angled her head and the sun reflected in her bright blue eyes. She lifted her hand to block it, waiting for him to continue. When he didn't, she asked, "Are you coming back?"

"I don't know yet."

Her smiled seemed strained. "You'll be missed around here."

Harrison bent his head and scratched his forehead. "I need to sort through some things. Put my parents' home up for sale." His brother had killed himself in the bathroom. He'd never be happy there, but he couldn't avoid going back. He had to sell the house and move on.

"That'll be good."

"I agree. It's long overdue. I've been paying someone to cut the grass, shovel the snow and do a walk-through every few weeks to make sure everything is okay. Like no busted pipes or a break-in. But enough of that. It's time I went back."

"I've learned you can't find your way forward until you make peace with the past." She raised her eyebrows. She spoke from experience.

"Keep me in your prayers," he said before he had a chance to overthink it. Slowly coming back to his faith had given him some direction and peace.

A light came into her eyes. "I will. I'm confident

you'll be fine." She took a few steps, then turned back around. "Don't be a stranger."

"I won't." But in truth, he wasn't sure what the future held.

EPILOGUE

Three weeks later...

Harrison slammed his locker door and twisted the combination lock. His arm had healed and he was allowed back at work. He had finished his first shift at the Quail Hollow Sheriff's Department, disappointed that he hadn't crossed paths with Becky. Maybe she had taken the day off.

He waved casually to a few fellow officers who were coming in for the second shift. When he had left Quail Hollow, he wasn't certain if he'd ever be back. Whether he'd see this place. These people. Sure, he had officially been out on disability, but in his heart, he knew there was a real possibility of calling in his resignation once he got bogged down with the details of settling his life in Buffalo.

Three weeks of cleaning out his family's home and sorting through all the possessions and memories gave him a lot of time to think. And most of his thoughts involved Becky Spoth.

After he had done his part to clear out his family's possessions, he had left the rest in the hands of a Realtor who would hold an estate sale and list the house. The rest could be managed by a quick visit to Buffalo to sign papers.

He had more important business in Quail Hollow.

Harrison pushed through the glass doors, and the afternoon heat hit his face. Soon, the temperatures would drop and everyone would be complaining about the cold.

He climbed into his truck and backed out. As he came around the corner, he noticed Becky's car parked where their adventures together first began. Curious, he slowed. Leaning forward against the steering wheel he searched for any sign of her.

A knocking on his side window startled him. He turned and saw Becky smiling at him. *Ah, that smile.* He pressed the lever to lower the window.

"Looking for someone?" she asked, a twinkle brightening her eyes.

"I thought maybe you had another flat."

"Oh, hush, things have finally settled down. Don't go trying to stir things up again."

Harrison held up his hands. "I wouldn't dream of it."

"I heard you were back."

"How?"

"Oh, a little birdie told me." He could only imagine. Word spread like wild fire in this small town.

"I had to be in court today."

"Anything to report?"

"Nothing I want to talk about. Time will settle everything." She rested her forearm on the ledge of his door. "I want to know about you. How's your arm?"

He held it up. "Good as new."

"And your trip home?"

"Good. I accomplished everything I needed to accomplish."

"Glad to hear it."

"You holding the fort down here?"

"Trying to. Rounded up the Hoffstettlers' cows that got out through a broken fence, gave a stern talking to some young boys who thought it would be more fun to steal a few apples from Mrs. Lapp's produce stand than pay for them…" She hitched up her shoulders. "You know, the usual fare."

"Sounds like things *are* back to normal."

"Yes, that's a very good thing." Becky stepped back from the door and jutted her lower lip to blow the hair off her face. Then she grew serious. "And you're back. I didn't know that you had plans to return."

"I didn't know myself when I left here. I did a lot of thinking while I was gone. I only got in late last night. I was due to report to work this morning." He studied her face. "I should have called you, but I wanted to talk to you in person."

"Oh?"

"I missed…this place." He didn't want to scare her off. They had agreed not to date, but he held out hope that perhaps they could revisit that possibility now that he was staying. But he didn't want to be presumptuous.

She raised her eyebrows in expectation. Her hair was pulled into a long ponytail with a few strands falling loosely around her face. "You missed this place, huh?"

He tilted his head to one side and studied her. "Yes, very much."

"Well, I think this place missed you, too," she said, pink blossoming on her cheeks. "And I thought maybe you'd like to hear about all the things you missed since you've been gone. Perhaps over dinner?"

"Dinner?" He smiled. "Something low key?"

"Absolutely low key. Tonight, if you're free."

He glanced at the clock on his truck dashboard. "I happen to be free." He kept his voice even.

"Great." She tucked her fingers into the back pockets of her pants. "See you in an hour."

"I look forward to it."

The doorbell rang and Becky quickly dried her hands on the dish towel after rinsing a cucumber for the salad. Chewie ran in circles and barked, probably more excited than she was. But unlike Chewie, Becky was going to play it down a little.

As she crossed the house to answer the door, she nervously wiped her hands on her capris. She had almost everything ready for dinner except for a few vegetables for the salad. She probably would have had everything ready except Chewie took his good old time getting around to doing his business outside.

Smoothing a hand down her top, she drew in a deep breath and leaned forward to open the door. Deputy Harrison James stood on her porch with a bouquet of wildflowers in his hand and a huge smile on his face. Her heart nearly exploded in her chest. In that moment she couldn't figure out why she had held him at arm's length for so long.

Well, she knew, but she also knew that events in life made you reevaluate your priorities. What you thought you wanted or didn't want could change a hundred times over a lifetime.

And then on one beautiful afternoon, God's plan lined everything up perfectly.

"Hello." He handed her the flowers. "For you."

She lifted the bouquet to her nose and inhaled. "They smell wonderful." She stepped back to allow room for him to enter.

"Whatever you're cooking smells wonderful, too."

"I have homemade chicken pot pies in the oven and I just finished mashing the potatoes. I learned how to cook as a child, but I haven't made some of my favorite meals in a long time." Ever since she had left the Amish, she had been exploring new things. She had lost sight of her past. No more. Leaving the Amish didn't mean she had to abandon her roots. "I was putting together a salad, but you caught me before I finished."

Harrison followed her to the kitchen while she pulled a vase out from under the counter and filled it with water from the utility sink. He went over to the kitchen sink and washed his hands, then picked up the cucumber. "Slices okay?"

"Um…" Becky jerked her head back. "You don't have to do that."

"I know I don't have to do that. I like cooking." He slid a sharp knife out of the butcher block. "This okay? On the cutting board here?"

"Sure."

While Harrison sliced the cucumbers and then the tomatoes, Becky poured lemonade and put the rest of the food on the table.

The doorbell rang and Becky glanced at Harrison as if he might know who was stopping by. She hustled to the front door, surprised to find her mother standing there.

"Hello, Rebecca," her mother said.

"Um…" Confusion swirled in Becky's head. She looked past her *mem* to find her *dat* sitting in the buggy, reins in hand.

"I didn't mean to stop unannounced." She shoved the bundle in her hand toward her daughter. "I thought you might like this for your home."

Becky glanced down and recognized the deep greens and soft yellows of a quilt she had started as a teen. The back of her nose tingled. She had left home before she had a chance to complete the project. She fingered the finished edges, then met her mother's steady gaze. "I hope you don't mind," her mother said. "Mag and I finished it for you. We thought you might like it in your home. Soon, the nights will be getting colder."

Becky hugged it to her chest. "Yes, thank you." Her mind drifted to the soft green she had used to paint her bedroom. "It will match my bedroom perfectly."

"Gut." Her mother dipped her head shyly.

"Would you like to come in?"

Her mother quickly shook her head. "No, your father and I are on our way home. Mag and Abram are expecting us." She turned to walk away, then turned back around. "Perhaps another time."

"Yes, perhaps." Becky lifted her hand to wave to her father and was rewarded with a tip of his hat.

Harrison came up behind her just as her mother was pulling herself back up on the wagon. She closed the door and set the quilt on a bench inside the door. "They dropped off a quilt I had started to make when

I was just a girl. My mother and sister took the time to finish it."

"That was nice."

"Yes, it was." She blinked away the emotions raining down on her. She fought to keep her voice from shaking. "I suppose we should eat."

"I put the salad on the table."

Becky dished out the rest of the meal and they sat down across from each other. "I'm glad you were free for dinner," she said. "I had all this food and no one to cook for."

Harrison took a bite of the flaky pastry on the pot pie. "Oh, wow, this is good."

"Thanks." For some reason, she suddenly felt shy.

"How has work been since you've been back?"

"Good," Becky said, happy to be on neutral ground. "The sheriff has come out with more promises to be transparent after he…"

"Wasn't transparent."

Becky laughed. "Exactly. He had his nephew's best interests at heart. The kid hadn't done anything wrong in Quail Hollow, but in light of everything else going on, it just threw a wrench into our investigation. But regardless, I think Sheriff Landry has survived to sheriff another day."

"People often have their judgment clouded by family." Harrison dipped his head and rubbed the back of his neck. "I was so angry at my brother for getting involved with drugs. For bringing shame on my family—the memory of my father and mother—that I wasn't there for him. But I've come to peace with everything that's happened. I've learned to have faith thanks to you."

"I'm happy you've found peace." Becky reached across the table and covered his hand. "Sometimes part of that process means you have to make your own family."

Becky was grateful her family had allowed the ice to melt, including giving her the beautiful quilt, but they'd never be one of those families who got together for Thanksgiving and shared laughter and naps during the football game. It could never be that way with them.

Harrison pushed back his chair and came around to her side of the table and pulled the chair out next to hers. He sat down on the edge and leaned toward her. "I'd like to think that maybe someday you'd consider me family."

Becky's heart raced as she met his steady gaze. She cleared her throat. "You've been there for me when I had no one else."

He cupped her cheek with his hand. He leaned in and pressed his lips to hers, warm and inviting. He pulled back and studied her face. "I have no plans to go anywhere, if that's all right with you?"

Butterflies fluttered in her belly at the intense gaze in his eyes. "You'd think someone who was adventurous enough to leave the Amish and start a new life wouldn't get so nervous when it came to change, even good change."

"You've had a lot of changes in your life." He was so close she could see flecks of yellow in his eyes. "And I suppose over the course of our lives, there will be many more."

"Whatever lies ahead, it's good to know I'm not alone. I'm glad you're here." It was her turn to lean closer and press a kiss to his lips. He tasted like a home-cooked meal and the promise of the future.

She felt his lips curve into a smile against hers. "Me, too."

* * * * *

If you enjoyed this book, look for some of the other great stories of suspense from Alison Stone, available now.

PLAIN JEOPARDY
PLAIN SANCTUARY
PLAIN COVER-UP
PLAIN PROTECTOR
PLAIN THREATS

Find more great reads at www.LoveInspired.com

Dear Reader,

Welcome back to Quail Hollow. When I start any new book series, I'm not always sure where I'll end up. During the writing process is when I get most of my best ideas. So when Deputy Becky Spoth strolled onto the page in *Plain Jeopardy* to protect Grace Miller, I immediately knew I had to tell her story. Becky had left her Amish home to become a sheriff's deputy in her hometown. It seemed like a tough path to follow, but she does it with grace and God's guidance. I hope you enjoyed her story.

I think, like Becky, many people choose to follow a path in life that is neither easy nor popular, but they know it is the one God wants them to be on. And when doubt swamps them, they have to learn to rely on their faith to guide them. Even if the path isn't difficult, some people struggle to know what God calls them to do. During my lifetime, I've prayed for guidance as I studied engineering, then became a full-time mom, then took up writing. Oftentimes I wondered if I was making the right decisions. But when I look around, I recognize my blessings and I am grateful. I also continue to pray for guidance.

As always, I truly appreciate my readers. Thank you. Please feel free to drop me a note at *Alison@ AlisonStone.com* or Alison Stone, PO Box 333, Buffalo, NY 14051.

Live, Love, Laugh,
Alison

COMING NEXT MONTH FROM
Love Inspired® Suspense

Available June 5, 2018

TOP SECRET TARGET
Military K-9 Unit • by Dana Mentink

Lieutenant Ethan Webb is ordered to protect his ex-wife from a serial killer, but when he and his K-9 partner arrive, he discovers that private investigator Kendra Bell is posing as the target. Ethan will have to draw out a killer without losing his heart.

VANISHED IN THE NIGHT
Wrangler's Corner • by Lynette Eason

After saving her from an attempted kidnapping and delivering her baby on the side of the road, Dr. Joshua Crawford feels responsible for Kaylee Martin and her newborn son. With danger dogging their every step, will he be able to protect this new family he has come to love?

HIDDEN AWAY
by Sharon Dunn

When Isabel Connor stumbles on a smuggling ring, her only choices are to run...or die. It's a struggle for her to trust anyone, yet undercover investigator Jason Enger is the only ally she has as she flees from danger—and finds herself heading straight into a deadly storm.

FATAL RECALL
by Carol J. Post

Paige Tatem is an amnesiac with a target on her back—and her survival depends on police officer Tanner Brody. Tanner doesn't know what she's forgotten, but he knows people will kill to ensure she never remembers—and it's up to him to stop them.

DANGEROUS OBSESSION
The Security Specialists • by Jessica R. Patch

Wilder Flynn, owner of a private security company, vows to protect Cosette LaCroix, his behavioral expert, from a stalker. But can he accomplish the mission without breaking his strict code against dating employees? Or revealing the deep, dark secrets he's held close all these years?

KILLER COUNTRY REUNION
by Jenna Night

After gunmen attack Caroline Marsh, she's stunned to still be alive—and bowled over that her rescuer is her ex-fiancé, Zane Coleman. The killers on her trail won't give up easily, and though Zane already left her once, for her own protection, he's not about to lose her again.

LOOK FOR THESE AND OTHER LOVE INSPIRED BOOKS WHEREVER BOOKS ARE SOLD, INCLUDING MOST BOOKSTORES, SUPERMARKETS, DISCOUNT STORES AND DRUGSTORES.

LISCNM0518

Get 4 FREE REWARDS!

We'll send you 2 FREE Books <u>plus</u> 2 FREE Mystery Gifts.

Love Inspired® Suspense books feature Christian characters facing challenges to their faith... and lives.

FREE Value Over **$20**

YES! Please send me 2 FREE Love Inspired® Suspense novels and my 2 FREE mystery gifts (gifts are worth about $10 retail). After receiving them, if I don't wish to receive any more books, I can return the shipping statement marked "cancel." If I don't cancel, I will receive 4 brand-new novels every month and be billed just $5.24 each for the regular-print edition or $5.74 each for the larger-print edition in the U.S., or $5.74 each for the regular-print edition or $6.24 each for the larger-print edition in Canada. That's a savings of at least 13% off the cover price. It's quite a bargain! Shipping and handling is just 50¢ per book in the U.S. and 75¢ per book in Canada*. I understand that accepting the 2 free books and gifts places me under no obligation to buy anything. I can always return a shipment and cancel at any time. The free books and gifts are mine to keep no matter what I decide.

Choose one: ☐ **Love Inspired® Suspense**
Regular-Print
(153/353 IDN GMY5)

☐ **Love Inspired® Suspense**
Larger-Print
(107/307 IDN GMY5)

Name (please print)

Address   Apt. #

City   State/Province   Zip/Postal Code

Mail to the **Reader Service:**
IN U.S.A.: P.O. Box 1341, Buffalo, NY 14240-8531
IN CANADA: P.O. Box 603, Fort Erie, Ontario L2A 5X3

Want to try two free books from another series? Call 1-800-873-8635 or visit www.ReaderService.com.

LIS18

SPECIAL EXCERPT FROM

Love Inspired
SUSPENSE

Ethan Webb is assigned as bodyguard to a woman impersonating his ex. Can they draw the killer out without losing their hearts?

Read on for a sneak preview of
TOP SECRET TARGET by **Dana Mentink**,
*the next book in the **MILITARY K-9 UNIT** miniseries,*
available June 2018 from Love Inspired Suspense!

First Lieutenant Ethan Webb brushed past the startled aide standing in Colonel Masters's outer office.

"The colonel is—"

"Waiting for me," Ethan snapped. "I know." Lt. Col. Terence Masters, Ethan's former father-in-law, was always a step ahead of him. He led Titus, his German shorthaired pointer, into the office, found Masters seated in his leather chair.

"You're late," Masters said. "And I don't want your dog in here."

"With respect, sir, the dog goes where I go, and I don't appreciate you pressuring my commanding officer to get me to do this harebrained job during my leave. I said I would consider it, didn't I?"

"A little extra insurance to help you make up your mind, Webb."

LISEXP0518

"It's a bad idea. Leave me alone to do my investigation with the team at Canyon, and we'll catch Sullivan." They were working around the clock to put away the serial killer who was targeting his air force brothers and sisters as well as a few select others, including Ethan's ex-wife, Jillian.

"Your team," Masters said, "hasn't gotten the job done, and this lunatic has threatened my daughter. You're going to work for me privately, protect Jillian from Sullivan, draw him out and catch him, as we've discussed."

"So you think I'm going to pretend to be married to Jillian again and that's going to put us in the perfect position to catch Sullivan?" He shoved a hand through his crew-cut hair, striving for control. "This is lunacy. I can't believe you're willing to use your daughter as bait."

"I'm not," he said. "I've decided it's too risky for Jillian, and that's why I hired this girl. This is Kendra Bell."

The civilian woman stepped into the office and Ethan could only stare at her.

"You're…" He shook himself slightly and tried again. "I mean… You look like…"

"Your ex-wife," she finished. "I know. That's the point."

Don't miss
TOP SECRET TARGET by Dana Mentink,
available June 2018 wherever
Love Inspired® Suspense books and ebooks are sold.

www.LoveInspired.com

Love Inspired®

Inspirational Romance to Warm Your Heart and Soul

Join our social communities to connect with other readers who share your love!

Sign up for the Love Inspired newsletter at **www.LoveInspired.com** to be the first to find out about upcoming titles, special promotions and exclusive content.

CONNECT WITH US AT:

Harlequin.com/Community

 Facebook.com/LoveInspiredBooks

 Twitter.com/LoveInspiredBks